Strange Beasties

Third Flatiron Anthologies
Volume 6, Book 20, Fall 2017

Edited by Juliana Rew
Cover Art by Keely Rew

Strange Beasties
Third Flatiron Anthologies
Volume 6, Fall 2017

Published by Third Flatiron Publishing
Juliana Rew, Editor and Publisher

Copyright 2017 Third Flatiron Publishing
ISBN #978-0-9990704-3-7

Discover other titles by Third Flatiron:
(1) Over the Brink: Tales of Environmental Disaster
(2) A High Shrill Thump: War Stories
(3) Origins: Colliding Causalities
(4) Universe Horribilis
(5) Playing with Fire
(6) Lost Worlds, Retraced
(7) Redshifted: Martian Stories
(8) Astronomical Odds
(9) Master Minds
(10) Abbreviated Epics
(11) The Time It Happened
(12) Only Disconnect
(13) Ain't Superstitious
(14) Third Flatiron's Best of 2015
(15) It's Come to Our Attention
(16) Hyperpowers
(17) Keystone Chronicles
(18) Principia Ponderosa
(19) Cat's Breakfast

License Notes

www.thirdflatiron.com

Contents

Foreword by Lizz-Ayn Shaarawi 7

In the Days of Mister Cuddles by Bruce Arthurs .. 11

Valediction by John Sunseri 23

The Wraith's Child by Philip John Schweitzer 35

Besta Branco by Tim Jeffreys 45

How Not to Eat People by Sarah Tchernev 55

To Riddle the Lake by Lucy Harlow 65

The Black Horse by Philip Brian Hall 73

Glass by Jean Graham 85

Creatures by Marc E. Fitch 93

Thirsty Creatures by Christa Carmen 103

Harry on the Farm by Isobel Horsburgh 109

Sailors' Hearts Taste Better
    by Paulo Da Silva 117

The Passenger by Jeff Hewitt 123

Beast of the Month by Wulf Moon 135

The Spark That Starts the Flame
    by Daniel Rosen 143

Niagwahe by Brenton Clark 153

Looking for Lusca by John J. Kennedy 163

Project Sargasso Findings on Global
    Nightmare Epidemic by Brian Trent 175

Credits and Acknowledgments 185

*****~~~~~*****

Strange Beasties, a Foreword

by Lizz-Ayn Shaarawi

Since the beginning of time, strange beasties have haunted the imagination. Whether seen as helpful or harmful, they've lurked in the shadows of the human psyche, peeking out when we least expect it. They are the reason early man gathered around the fire and feared the dark. They are the reason grandmothers warned youngsters to stay on the path and to never venture into the shadowy forest alone. Stories of beasties have been instrumental throughout history, the means by which we are taught important lessons of survival, lessons of morality, and lessons of courage.

The stories curated for the *Strange Beasties* anthology span a wide variety of creatures from the tame to the terrible. Frightening monstrosities and blood curdling tales fill the following pages alongside majestic beasts and uplifting yarns.

Not all the strange beasties in these tales mean harm. In the opening story, "In the Days of Mister Cuddles" by Bruce Arthurs, a young girl from an eccentric family brings home a new pet from the multi-dimensional woods behind her house. In "How Not to Eat People" by Sarah Tchernev, a podcast produced by monsters, for monsters, tries to help beasties assimilate in the human world. Two kindred spirits enjoy the last day of a race track and the noble creatures that compete there in "Valediction" by John Sunseri. On a freezing night at a hot spring, the death and life of an old god and a middle-aged human intertwine in "The Passenger" by Jeff Hewitt.

At times, human hunters can be more beastly than the creatures they stalk, as in the tale "The Spark That

Starts the Flame" by Daniel Rosen, where a man tracks down a marginal species his past actions have harmed. "Besta Branco" by Tim Jeffreys tells of three western hunters who discover a greater threat than they bargained for when they hunt a mythical beast of the Amazon.

Motherhood takes the forefront in a trio of stories, though whether maternal instinct helps or hinders the characters changes with each tale. In "Creatures" by Marc E. Fitch, a predator that mimics a crying child is captured by a group of scientists. "The Wraith's Child" by Philip Schweitzer tells of a wraith, infertile in life, who decides, in death, to take matters into her own hands. The chilling tale "Niagwahe" by Brenton Clark is of a cabin in the woods, where a young family comes face to face with a creature of the forest best known in native folk tales.

Harking back to classic legends, some of the beasties here exist to punish those who transgress. In "The Black Horse" by Philip Brian Hall, hubris turns an aristocrat's wager into a race for his soul, whereas in "Glass" by Jean Graham, a murderer forced to return to the scene of his crime discovers his just rewards have been waiting for him.

Not all beasties are born fierce creatures. Some take time to reach their full potential. Isobel Horsburgh's story "Harry on the Farm" tells of a boy and his father who take a drive to drop his beloved puppy off at a farm in the country. In "Sailors' Hearts Taste Better" by Paulo Da Silva, an ancient mermaid tries to lure a young fresh water siren to the sea so that she can embrace her true nature. The lone survivor of an apocalypse changes with her surroundings in "Thirsty Creatures" by Christa Carmen.

Not all of the stories contained here prove horrific and terrifying. "Beast of the Month" by Wulf Moon is a humorous story of a subscription service for wizards gone wrong, told in escalating correspondence.

Foreword

Humans are not always the intended targets, as in "To Riddle the Lake" by Lucy Harlow, where nature provides terrifying creatures born of itself. Fire and water fight and come together, split and evolve in beautiful and frightening prose.

"Looking for Lusca" by John J. Kennedy tells of a scuba diver who finds a creature in the murky depths that helps him reach his full potential through visions and blackouts, though at a price he's not sure he wants to pay. In "Project Sargasso Findings on Global Nightmare Epidemic" by Brian Trent, dreams hold the key to human survival.

The Strange Beasties found in these stories exist to terrify and delight, to remind us that the darkness is closer than we realize. So, don't check the noise just outside the window that lures you into the night beyond the glass. Ignore the creak of the floorboards above that sounds suspiciously like footsteps. Pay no attention to the skittering under the bed or the dark shape that flits from view at the corner of your eye. Sit back, stay close to the light, and enjoy the following tales.

Lizz-Ayn Shaarawi
August 2017

*****~~~~~*****

In The Days Of Mister Cuddles

by Bruce Arthurs

Athena Menlo brought home a cat. Five-year-olds do that sort of thing. She found the cat in the very deep woods at the back of her family's very large backyard, behind her family's very large house, which lay back from an even larger front yard. The woods were so deep they held more than a usual wood. They held three hundred thirty-three-and-a-third woods and worlds that existed in three hundred thirty-three-and-a-third overlapping planes of existence. Those worlds were packed in so tightly that only a very few very special people could walk into them or see beyond the top layer.

Being Athena Menlo, who was smarter than her very smart father Aloysius Menlo, and more talented than her very talented mother Hypatia Menlo, and more special than her very ordinary older sister Jane, the cat she carried home was more than a cat.

"Father, I have brought home a cat. It shall be my cat, my very own cat."

"That's nice, Athena," said Aloysius Menlo, turning from the walls of his chalkboard-lined study to spare Athena an indulgent glance. "But that is not a cat. Cats do not have so many legs." Aloysius Menlo was a genius with numbers. His brain had three hemispheres instead of the usual two, so he could hold far more thoughts in his head than normal people. He had six

11

fingers on each hand and six toes on each foot, letting him think in twenty-four dimensions. His calculatory skill was in high demand and higher remuneration from people who could not understand his results.

Athena stamped her foot. "Is too a cat!" she cried. "It is *my* cat!" But her father had already turned back to his chalkboards and was chalking furiously.

Athena went to her mother's studio. "Mother, I have brought home a cat. It shall be my cat, my very own cat."

"That's nice, dear," said Hypatia Menlo, turning from her easel to spare Athena an indulgent glance. "But that is not a cat. Cats do not have so many eyes." Hypatia Menlo knew eyes. Her own were exceptional. She could see in infrared and ultraviolet. She could see the color of the nothingness that existed before the Big Bang. (No, that's not black. Black is far too bright and vibrant to ever compare.) She could see the color at the center of the Sun. (No, that's not white. White is too dull and lifeless to compare.) She could see the color of time; she could see the color of memory; she could see the colors of hope and despair. And all these colors (or, at least, their best possible imitations, for some colors are inimitable) Hypatia Menlo put into her canvases, works in high demand, at high remuneration, by people whose own vision was stunted and frozen within normal limits.

Athena stamped her foot. "Is too a cat! Is *my* cat!" But her mother had already turned back to the easel and was painting furiously.

Athena went to her sister Jane's room. "Jane, I have brought ho—"

"*Jumping Jimmy Jehoshaphat on a jungle gym!*" cried Jane, leaping from her chair onto the bed and backing into a corner of the room, her average-looking eyes wide in her average-looking face. "*You're holding a giant spider!*"

"Is not! It's a cat! It is *my* cat!"

12

"It has eight long legs and eight huge creepy eyes!"

"It's an eight-legged, eight-eyed cat!"

"I don't care what you call it! It's the size of a sack of potatoes, with bristly fur and big fangs! Get it out of my room!"

Athena stamped her foot. "You're jealous because I have a cat and you don't!"

"I don't want a cat! I want a normal sister, and normal parents, and a normal life!"

It was too late for that, of course. Jane's misfortune was to be solidly average in all regards. She was somewhere on the bell curve. Her parents and sister weren't on the curve at all. It made Jane's life an unhappy one. Not horribly unhappy. Not terribly unhappy. Just. . . averagely unhappy, an average amount of the time. Right now, Jane was a little more unhappy than that. Right now, Jane's insufferable younger sister had brought a giant spider, a giant *hairy* spider, into Jane's bedroom.

It was the sort of thing Athena did. Athena's own singular talent lay in taking, not the road less traveled, but roads no one else saw at all. At the edge of the woods behind the sprawling Menlo manse, normal people might see spiders, with webs and trapdoors or walking solitary like hobos, but certainly no giant ones. But Athena could see, and walk into, the three hundred thirty-three-and-a-third worlds in that spot, overlapping in such ways only the topmost layer was visible to most people. That's how universes work, but ordinary people aren't able to figure that out.

Aloysius Menlo and his chalkboards had calculated the existence of three hundred thirty-three of those worlds, but that remaining one-third of a world stumped him. He couldn't get his numbers straight for that last bit, no matter how many boxes of chalk he used. It annoyed him; it irritated him; it frustrated him; it vexed him and hexed him. When he snapped the last piece of chalk from the last box of chalk in two, he threw up his hands and went to ask his daughter.

"What's up with this last one-third of the three hundred thirty-three-and-a-third worlds, daughter? I can't get my numbers to work out. My quadratic equations not only don't equate, they won't even quad. That never happens."

"Why are you asking me?" replied Jane. "I'm just averagely intelligent. Ask Athena. She's smarter than all of us."

Jane might have been average, but her answer sounded pretty darned smart to Aloysius. "Gosh!" he exclaimed. "That's right! I have another daughter!" Aloysius was great at keeping track of very large and very complicated numbers, not so great at keeping track of his children. Who can blame him? Chalk did not write well on his daughters' skin.

So Aloysius Menlo and Jane went to Athena and asked. "Athena, what's up with this last one-third of a world beside the three hundred thirty-three invisible worlds you visit?"

"Oh, I never visit *that* world, Daddy," Athena had replied. "If I ever went there, only a third of me would come back. And the woods aren't invisible, you only have to have good enough eyes to see them."

(Hypatia Menlo's eyes were good enough to see a wisp of a trace of a ghost of the extra worlds when she looked hard enough. But some of the colors on some of the worlds hurt Hypatia's eyes and upset her stomach. Some of the colors made her toes curl, and not in the good direction toes are supposed to curl. So Hypatia tried not to look in that direction.)

"Did you bring that stupid spider back from one of those stupid invisible worlds?" asked Jane.

"They're not invisible. And they're not stupid, either." That wasn't strictly true. One world was so dumb

14

it thought it was just a world and never spoke to anyone. "But yes, my cat came from one of them."

"Take it back!"

"No! It is my cat, and I have named it Mister Cuddles, and I will keep him, so there!" And Athena stamped her foot and left, taking Mister Cuddles with her.

Weeks passed, and the rest of Athena's family, except Jane, grew used to Mister Cuddles. The disappearance of the big house's occasional bugs even made Mister Cuddles slightly appreciated.

Aloysius Menlo spoke to Athena one day around then. "You haven't seen my lab mice, have you? Several seem to have escaped their maze." The maze he was referring to was his own invention. Instead of remembering twists and turns, mice had to remember numbers. Several mice had mastered the multiplication tables, but they all seemed to get stuck in a corner at trigonometry, and calculus just made them shiver and cry. "And by the way, your odd-looking cat seems larger than I remembered."

Athena laid down the shears she was using to cut a large piece of heavy leather. "Oh, Daddy, Mister Cuddles isn't a cat."

"Really? You seemed very certain."

"No! He's actually a *kitten*, silly."

"I see. Perhaps I shall purchase stronger locks for the maze room, and stronger cages for the mice."

Several weeks after that, Hypatia Menlo spoke to Athena.

"Athena, dear, do you have any idea where all the garden birds have gone? I was thinking of painting some nature portraits. And oh my, Mister Cuddles has certainly grown."

Athena laid down the stout curved needle and heavy waxed thread she was using to stitch heavy leather pieces over a wooden frame shaped like a large oblong doughnut. "The birds were awfully noisy, Mother. Isn't it more peaceful without them?"

"I suppose you have a point," said Hypatia, who went back to her studio to paint imaginary birds feathered in imaginary colors instead.

And several weeks after that, Jane rushed into Athena's room.

"Athena! What did you do? The entire neighborhood is on the march. Again! They have torches and pitchforks. Again! And this time the torches are actually li— *Holy Mother Mary on a soda cracker!* Is that Mister Cuddles? *Why is he wearing a saddle?*"

"Ummmm. . . " began Athena. But Aloysius and Hypatia burst into the room.

"Athena!" Aloysius exclaimed. "The neighbors have torches and pitchforks!"

"Again!" exclaimed Hypatia.

"And this time the torches are lit! What did you do, Athena?"

". . . mmmmm," continued Athena, looking anywhere but at her parents or sister.

"It *might* have something to do with the 'LOST DOG' and 'LOST CAT' fliers posted around the neighborhood," Jane volunteered.

Remember now, Athena Menlo is a very smart five-year-old. So Athena did the smartest thing a five-year-old can do: She began to cry. Great wails and sobs, copious tears, and a face flushed scarlet.

"Oh, honey, don't cry," said Hypatia.

"Everything will be all right, sweetie," said Aloysius.

"You manipulative little booger," said Jane. Jane had spent a year as a five-year-old once, and she remembered all the tricks.

Athena stopped crying and glared at Jane. "You poopyhead," she replied.

"I hear shouting," said Hypatia.

16

"I smell burning," said Aloysius.

"*Saint Sebastian in a salad spinner!* I guess I've got to deal with this myself." Jane took a step towards Mister Cuddles, stopped, shivered, then squared her shoulders and moved forward again.

"Hey, that's *my* cat! And *my* saddle! Get off him!"

But Jane had already climbed into Mister Cuddles's saddle and taken up the reins. "Giddyup!" she cried, and the eight-legged, eight-eyed giant creature we will call a cat for courtesy's sake obeyed. Aloysius, Hypatia, and Athena jumped aside as steed and rider left Athena's room. Jane ducked to avoid bonking her head on the doorframe, Mister Cuddles squooshed itself narrower to fit through, and they galloped down the long hallway towards the front entrance.

Aloysius, Hypatia, and Athena followed, stopping in the front room. Through the tall, wide windows they could see the mob of neighbors running back and forth in panic, tossing away torches and pitchforks. Through the open front door, they could hear the screaming as Jane and Mister Cuddles drove them first one way, then another. Mister Cuddles clacked his mandibles and occasionally reared up to wave the claws of his front legs menacingly, until the mob finally retreated to the street and ran away down it, still screaming.

"Was our eldest daughter *herding* our neighbors off our property?"

"I believe she was. You know, I've always thought we had an excessively large lawn. Perhaps we should get sheep for it."

"That would be cool!" Athena said. "Mister Cuddles and I could be sheepherders!"

The last of the former mob vanished down the street, although the sound of screams still drifted in the air another moment or two before fading away. Jane and Mister Cuddles rode back into the front room of the house.

17

"Are you all right, Jane?" Jane's parents asked as Jane swung out of the saddle and back to the ground.

"I rode on top of a giant, hairy, disgusting hypertrophied arachnid," Jane said, then paused for a second, looking thoughtful. "Actually. . . it was kind of fun."

"We're getting a flock of sheep!" Athena was so excited she forgot to hate her sibling. "We're all going to be sheepherders!"

"Well, that problem's solved." Aloysius Menlo was fidgeting with a piece of chalk, eager to get back to his chalkboards and numbers.

"It's a nice day after all," said Hypatia Menlo. "Perhaps a painting is in order."

Jane rolled her eyes. "I'm doomed to be the practical member of an impractical family. Athena, the neighbors became upset because Mister Cuddles has been eating the neighborhood pets, hasn't he?"

"Mmmmm. . . maybe." Athena tried to look innocent; the effort failed.

"Has Mister Cuddles gotten his full growth yet? How big do spiders get on that phantom world he came from?"

"Mmmmm. . . maybe not. Mmmmm. . . pretty big?"

"So if Mister Cuddles gets bigger, he'll want to eat bigger animals. Like, say, people?"

"It'll be okay! I'd only let him eat people I don't like!"

Jane turned towards Aloysius and Hypatia. "Mom-m-m-m. Dad-d-d-d. You need to be *parents* here."

That made Aloysius and Hypatia break into cold sweats. But they rallied themselves and did the necessary thing.

This time when Athena cried, there was no fakery about it. She cried, while her parents talked. She wailed, while the family and Mister Cuddles walked to the woods

18

where three hundred thirty-three-and-a-third planes of existence overlapped. She sobbed, while Jane unsaddled Mister Cuddles.

"Athena, dear, you need to send Mister Cuddles back to the world he came from now." Hypatia squinted while she spoke, brow furrowed and her face a little green. The more exotic colors Hypatia could see in the woods were giving her a headache and nausea. Thankfully, her toes were still straight and in the right order.

"I don't want to," Athena sniffled.

"But you need to," said Jane.

"Hey, this close, I can see that one-third of a world that's been frustrating my calculations. Wow, it's a narrow darn thing." Aloysius reached out a hand towards the edge of the woods.

"Don't, Daddy!" Athena cried, alarmed. There was a *snip* sound from the air above.

Aloysius snatched his hand back, then looked at his fingertips. "Well, look at that. It gave me a manicure. Huh." He looked thoughtful for a moment, then his face brightened. "Aha! That's what I've been missing." He took a notepad and pencil from a pocket and began scribbling numbers and equations at a rapid pace.

Jane crouched down in front of her sister and put her hands on Athena's shoulders. "We know you don't want to give up Mister Cuddles. But he's getting too big and too hungry to keep, Athena. You need to do the responsible thing, even if you're only five."

"I don't wanna be 'sponsible. Why do I need to be 'sponsible?"

"Because if you grew up irresponsible, it would end with cities in ruins, civilization destroyed, and you ruling the shambling mutated survivors from atop a pile of skulls."

"Skulls are cool."

"No one wants to play with a little girl who collects skulls."

19

"They don't?"

"No."

"Oh." Athena stared dejectedly at the ground for a long moment, then drew in a deep breath and looked up again. "Okay. But can I get another cat?"

"As long as it's a *cat* cat this time," Hypatia answered.

Athena considered for a moment. "All right. Come on, Mister Cuddles."

Athena led the giant spider to the wood's edge. She flicked her fingers at the air as if through the pages of a book. The air rippled like heat waves above a bed of live coals. Athena's fingers slowed, then stopped. Hypatia looked away, her eyes crossing and pupils dilating, and rubbed her temples. Aloysius was still deep in his calculating and didn't look up. But Jane, even plain ordinary Jane (who, perhaps, was no longer quite so ordinary, for how many ordinary girls ever ride a giant spider?), caught a flash of another world, a world where titanic spiderwebs stretched between Sequoia-sized trees and many, many large arachnid eyes watched from deep within shadowed foliage. Then Jane's eyes stopped believing what they were seeing, and the spider-world went invisible again like the other three hundred thirty-three (and a third) worlds Athena could see and enter.

"Go on, Mister Cuddles." Athena said. Her voice was like a heart being ripped in two, and if you've ever heard a heart being ripped in two, you know it's a sound hard to listen to. "It's your home. Go on home."

The monstrous spider turned its head and looked at Athena with eight black unblinking eyes for several long seconds, then scuttled forward into the spider-world's space. As it crossed the edge of the woods, spider and spider-world faded away.

Jane and Hypatia heaved sighs of relief. Aloysius glanced up from his notepad and looked around. "Oh, are we done? Good."

Athena sniffled again and wiped her nose, then leaned down and lifted Mister Cuddles's saddle, holding it awkwardly in her arms. "Let's go home."

"Do you need help to carry that?" Jane asked.

"No."

"Are you keeping the saddle to remember Mister Cuddles?" Hypatia asked.

"Oh, no," Athena answered. "You said I could have a cat, if it was a *cat* cat." She heaved the saddle up onto one shoulder and started walking back towards the house.

"I think this will fit a tiger."

###

About the Author

Bruce Arthurs has been writing occasional stories since 1975, with over a dozen published in scattered venues over scattered years. After a long hiatus, he began writing fiction again in 2012 while recovering from a badly broken arm. He has also edited two anthologies, and he wrote an episode of Star Trek: The Next Generation ("Clues", 4th Season, 1991). His most recent published story, "Beks and the Second Note" (*ALFRED HITCHCOCK MYSTERY MAGAZINE*, December 2016) was a Best Short Story nominee for the 2017 Derringer short mystery fiction awards. He lives in Arizona with his wife Hilde, several housemates, and four cats.

*****~~~~~*****

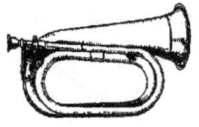

Valediction

by John Sunseri

They were shutting down the track. It was a long, slow, drawn-out death, but the track was going to die, and even though Ace didn't particularly want to watch something he loved sink into oblivion, he didn't see that he had much of a choice. He'd been there practically since the beginning. He'd be there for the end.

He leaned on the railing in his usual spot, about a third of a circuit from the starting gates. Back in the sixties he'd had to get there early, long before the first post time, to get a perch on the fence. Now he had his pick of places. There was a desultory crowd milling around, but no one seemed to want to get up close and personal. A kid, that was it—a girl, maybe twelve years old, with a program sticking out of the pocket of her jacket as she did push-ups on the iron rail to bleed off some of her energy while waiting for the race to start. Around her blew the stub ends of losing tickets, candy wrappers, cigarette butts, swirling in eddies of autumn wind. Ace wondered where her parents were.

Up in the skybox, probably, getting a drink, he thought. A seven-dollar beer for the gentleman, a glass of five-dollar plonk for the lady, and a few minutes up in the Premiere Lounge without the kid. Cheaper than a night at the movies, with the benefit of fresh air for the girl.

Ace chewed on the butt-end of his unlit cigar. He didn't smoke anymore. He'd had a rough run-in with lung cancer about ten years back, and it had left him skeletal and worn-out and old and irradiated, but it hadn't left him dead. He still liked the taste of the Romeo y Julieta in his mouth, though, and the weight of it between his teeth. The fact that the cigar-chewing old coot on the racetrack rail was a stereotype bothered him not at all. He'd been a cigar-chewing YOUNG coot, back when, and he'd aged into the trope gradually and gracefully.

He looked out over the track. The rich brown dark of the earth, the lush green of the grass in the middle of the oval, the sharp white pricks of the spotlights, and the lowering gray of the Portland skies painted another in a long line of hazy memories for him. He was getting to the point when he couldn't remember individual days with any detail, but his brain was stuffed with artistic composites. Tonight would be another added to the mosaic, another gloomy, windy, cool beautiful evening at the track, all whirling together in an old man's mind to make the one, perfect, Platonic night.

"What happens to the slugs when they can't race anymore?" asked the little girl.

Ace turned to look at her. Her face was serious.

"They send them to the salt mines," he said, gravely.

They looked at each other for a few pregnant seconds, then he smiled. "Just kidding, sweetheart."

She didn't look convinced. "Do they kill them?"

Art turned away, looked back at the track. They were bringing the slugs out for the first race, pulling on the harnesses, coaxing them with sugar and slaps, and he felt the familiar thrill that he always felt, watching the animals with their colors moving toward the starting line. The air was crisp, there was a smell of barbecue in the wind, and the track's speakers were playing the Colonel Bogey March as the racers slimed their way toward the

24

track, wrangled by their handlers, colors bright under the lights.

"Not all of them," he said, finally. "Some go to stud."

The little girl nodded, as though she'd expected the answer. She turned back to the fence to watch the parade of animals go by. Ace suddenly wished he had a match. Back in the day he'd enjoyed puffing on his Cubans as the slugs got jostled into their stalls, and he felt a strong, sudden pang of desire to go back to those days. There would be couples pushed up against him, giggling and laughing, waving team colors. There would be the cynical hacks shuffling money in the pockets of their slacks and worriedly scanning the slugs for signs of injury or sloth. Vendors would be shoving their way through the crowds, pregnant with flats of beer cups and bags of peanuts, hawking their wares to the receptive crowds. And there would be Ace Atcheson, dressed sharp in gabardine and patent leathers, silk socks and silk boxers, soaking it all in, billows of cigar smoke mingling with the clouds of conversation and anticipation in the autumn air.

"Who do you have for this race?" he asked, realizing as he asked the question that he was being an idiot. He was talking to a grade-school girl as though she was a punter, as though she knew anything about the business.

"Black Francis," she responded, still staring out at the slugs as they oozed into their stalls.

Ace nodded. Black Francis was the favorite. A big monster, with twelve wins already under his belt, and not a lot of competition tonight. There were one or two other slugs that might give him a chase, but it would be an upset if he lost. The numbers on the board showed that—the rest of the field was going to pay at least three to one, and possibly more, should something weird happen. But no one was betting on the rest of the field.

"Do they enjoy this?" the little girl asked, turning again to look at Ace. "Do they like racing?"

"Yes," said Ace. And he meant it. It was why he'd loved the sport in the first place. His gambler's soul could have been content with poker, or blackjack, or the stock market. But his heart had found happiness with the slugs. "They're meant for this. It's in their blood. They're meant to race."

"I'm Amanda," said the girl. She still didn't smile, though Ace knew that when and if she ever did, it would be transformative—she had that kind of face, a face that, when wreathed with a smile, would eventually cause men to destroy their lives for her. He'd known grifters that would have killed for a little girl with that kind of face, to pull in the suckers and their wallets.

"Ace," he said.

"You've got a slug in the sixth," she said. "Ace of Spades."

"Slow son of a bitch," nodded Ace. "He'll be lucky to finish in the top five."

"Might be worth a ten-spot, though," said Amanda. "Long shots sometimes come in."

Ace stopped chewing on his cigar and looked down at her with something like wonder on his face. "Are you really a kid?" he asked. "I mean, what the hell? You sound like a tout."

"My dad was a slug breeder," she said, shrugging. "He used to say that sometimes passion was stronger than blood."

Ace opened his mouth to reply, but at that moment the gun went off, and the slugs squeezed their way out of their gates. Black Francis was by far the biggest and strongest of them, but he got caught in an oozy scrum at the starting line, and by the time he shook off the two smaller slugs that had crashed into him, the leaders were three lengths ahead. Slime spattered like rain, and the moaning groans of the racing animals echoed in the canyon of the track like thunder. Ace felt his heart thrumming like drums, a thrumming that had nothing to do with cancer or age or ill health, and everything to do with love and excitement and sport, and he spun around to watch the slugs make the first turn.

The leader was a beast from Tri-Cities called Krazy Kougar, a sleek black slug smoothly chewing up the track, maybe five feet tall at its tallest stretch, wearing the red and silver of the third lane. It undulated and ululated and cruised along on the rail, argent slime glistening behind it as it went, and it looked absolutely beautiful as it whipped by Ace and Amanda, plasm hunching and bunching and propelling, and the crowd (such as it was) applauded its efforts. Ace looked back, though, toward the rest of the racers, and saw that Black Francis wasn't impressed by his competitor—the favorite was catching up already, having scattered three or four lesser animals in his glutinous wake and churning ahead like Moby Dick fixed on the *Pequod*. The gap was a body-length and a half, and there were still 500 yards to race.

"Francis has this," said Ace.

"Yeah," agreed Amanda.

You got so you could tell what was probably going to happen, if you paid enough attention and watched enough races. There were surprises, which is why they raced the slugs in the first place, but if you were a true student of the sport you could make a little money at it. Most people put their ten bucks on the slug that looked the most impressive, or had the cutest name, or wore the right colors. Guys like Ace—and, apparently, girls like Amanda—waited for things to get as sure as they could get (and it was nice when no one else could see those things, to drive up the odds), and then plunged the big bucks.

You couldn't make a fortune on it, unless you had connections to outside bookmakers (read: the Mob). Portland Meadows had a 500 dollar limit on bets. You could spread a few of those around, hitting different windows with different people that you trusted, but you still weren't going to walk out of the place a millionaire unless you'd walked in almost a millionaire. Some of Ace's compatriots, people he'd spent decades leaning on the rail with, had finally gotten discouraged after never hitting the big score and drifted on to other arenas, poker games, Vegas, places where you might, if Lady Luck grabbed you in the groin at just the right time, be able to retire wealthy.

Not, thought Ace, that any of them would ever retire. Gambling was their meat, their booze, their sex, their survival. They'd give it up as soon as they'd give up oxygen. For Ace it had always been different; his passion was for the race itself, the slugs churning in their lanes as they were doing now, the smell of hot dogs and slime and churned earth, the thrum of excitement from the crowd, the roars and curses, the torn-up tickets and the blare of the Colonel Bogey March as the racers were coaxed into their gates.

They were in the homestretch now. It was down to Black Francis and Krazy Kougar, and Francis was neck-and-neck with the former frontrunner, and starting to pull ahead. The crowd loved it—cheers cavalcaded through the grandstand, echoing in the bowl of the arena, urging one slug or the other forward, imprecating them, imploring them, and finally in the din and the chill air and the waft of smoke and fryer oil and musk, Black Francis pulled forward and surged over the finish line a full body length ahead.

"You have any money on this one?" asked Ace.

"I look like I'm old enough to bet?" said Amanda, her fists gripped tight on the flaked paint of the rail, her eyes gleaming with some kind of kid emotion Ace was way too old to identify. He smiled.

"They're amazing," she said as the last few slugs finally crossed the finish line and the trainers started wading into the pools of dirt and slime to corral them, coax them back into the tunnel, down into the subterranean holding pens to await their long truck rides to the next track—or to the slaughterhouses. Portland was a small market, and if the racers couldn't make it here, they weren't gonna make it in Tulsa or Scranton or at Churchill Downs. "They're so powerful. . . "

"I saw one of them knock over a semi truck once," said Ace. She turned her head, looked up into his face, and her eyes stopped gleaming and got pinprick interested. "It got loose for a couple seconds, and the handlers couldn't wrangle it back, and it slammed into one of the transport trucks at full speed after, hell, ten yards. You can't imagine the sound it made."

"Was the slug okay?" she asked.

He snorted. "Fine as paint," he said. "Those things are pure muscle. The truck tipped over onto nine wheels for a second, then crashed down into the ground, but the slug—its name was Conqueror, which was perfect—just shrunk back for a second, then started to haul ass in another direction. The handlers caught up with it, though, and lassoed it pretty quick. Good thing, too. It was ready to go do some more knocking over."

Amanda smiled. "I wish I would have seen it. Stupid truck."

Ace found himself smiling as well. "Stupid truck," he agreed. "Where the hell are your parents, anyway?"

"Mom's at work," she said. "I snuck in tonight. They say the track is shutting down next week, and I wanted to see."

Ace goggled, then composed himself. "Okay, then," he said, finally. "So you're at a racetrack by yourself in the middle of the night. . . "

"It's eight o'clock," she said.

". . . surrounded by hardened gamblers and bookies and probably pimps. . . "

29

"Were you a trainer?" she asked. "Or maybe an owner?"

He looked down at her for a couple breaths, then shook his head. "No. I was never in the business. But I always loved the slugs."

She nodded, and in her eyes Ace saw that she understood him perfectly. He'd snuck into a track or two, back when he was running numbers on the north side and picking the occasional pocket. It was a more peaceful era now, and the mobs had gotten out of the petty cash business and into the garbage industry, and the produce warehouses, and the nightclub racket, but Ace thought that Amanda would have made a hell of a runner in different times.

"It happened outside the Meadows," he said. "I've been coming here for a long time, and I, uh. . . " He stopped, then smiled again and flipped up his coat to reveal a keychain hanging from his belt. "I managed to get hold of some master keys. I wanted to see the stuff the crowds never see. I wanted to go down into the cages between races and watch them get fed, have their colors put on. I never wanted to be a trainer, or an owner, or a gambler. I just. . ."

"You just love the slugs," she finished.

"Yeah," he said, letting his coat drop back down, looking out at the track where the slugs for the second race were bulging forward. "Yeah. I just loved the slugs."

They were silent for a long moment. The music started again. Soon after, the second race started.

. . .

"Thank you," said Amanda, after the last race had been run, and as everyone was starting to file out.

"For what?" asked Ace.

"For telling me all the stories. For talking to a kid."

"It's a little creepy," said Ace. "I shouldn't be hanging out with a grade-school girl. If your mother was here, she'd probably want to kick my ass."

She laughed, and again he saw that smile. He'd felt *comfortable* with her all night, as though they were buddies from the same neighborhood rather than an old creak and a young weirdo, and though he'd been in the grip of a nostalgic melancholy for long weeks, waiting for the Meadows to die, her smile actually made him happy. The track would close, the slugs would scatter and most of them would die, and he'd have a hole in his life that he'd have trouble filling with anything else. But there was still passion in the world, and there were still kids growing up appreciating the beauty and the artistry of the Sport of Kings.

"Yeah," she said, her smile slowing. "She probably would."

"I'll walk you home," he said.

The smile came back. "The neighbors would love that. Some random old guy dropping me off after a night out. I only live a few blocks away. I'll be fine. But. . . Ace?"

"Yeah?" he said.

"Maybe a quick hug?"

He suppressed the quick terror he felt. But there were still plenty of people around. Witnesses, to say that he wasn't some creeper trying to take advantage of a kid. Then he leaned down and patted her back as she gave him, yes, a quick hug. They released, she smiled, and said, "See you around." Turned and walked away.

He stood there a while longer, then took out another cigar, stuck it into his mouth. He stared out at the track while the workers began to move out onto the concourses, onto the apron, and start sweeping. It was chilly now, but he was reluctant to go home. He wanted to make the moment last.

Moments never last, though. He hitched up his pants, shrugged deeper into his jacket, and started walking toward the exit.

...

31

The streets were silent but for the occasional whir of distant traffic and the electric click of the walk signals and traffic lights as they did their middle-of-the-night cycles. And the heels of Ace's shoes, staccato on the sidewalk as he walked home. He chewed on his cigar and felt the breeze on his face and wondered what he'd be doing in a couple of months during his evenings. Drinking, probably. Watching television. Remembering rather than living.

And then a crash behind him. He spun around, looked down the street, back the way he'd come.

Black Francis was there, surging, pulsing, in the middle of the road. Behind him was a coterie of nine or ten other slugs, all questing forward, moving in nine or ten other directions, all of them giddy with freedom, and they started slamming into telephone poles and parked cars, setting off alarms, knocking down stop signs, racing across intersections, bleating with glee.

The cigar dropped from Ace's jaws, bounced on the concrete.

Francis hesitated, vibrating in the cold night air, and then stretched his neck up, his antennae waving around, tasting the new experience. Around him pulsed the rest of the slugs that had raced tonight, a hundred of them, all moving fast and brutal and free, knocking chocks out of buildings, crunching locked bicycles into the pavement, roiling and rolling and roistering and, most of all, *racing*. It was in their blood. They moved fast, fast as the wind, and Ace windmilled himself back into a doorway as three of them whipped by, trailing slime that glistened in the streetlamps like diamonds, making their grunting noises that sounded, if you had ears to hear it, like cries of sheer ecstasy, as though they were back in the prairies in the days before the humans had come to tame them, roaming through the world free and unfettered.

Ace cautiously leaned forward after they passed, and saw more and more of the giant shapes moving

32

through the streets, and he ripped his jacket open to look at his belt.

The keys were gone. The keys that opened every door, of every stall in the Meadows.

"Quick hug my *ass*!" he roared, laughing, spinning, bending over to grab his knees. His heart hurt, but it was a *good* hurt, and he finally let himself lean back against the wall, slowly sink down until his bony old ass hit the pavement, and he just kept laughing and laughing and laughing.

The sirens were starting now. Lights were coming on in windows. People were starting to poke their heads out of windows and cautiously open doors. Dogs were barking. And Ace pulled himself back upright and just walked out of his doorway. There was a bar down the street. They'd have matches. And they'd have whiskey.

He was going to toast Amanda, have a drink, have a smoke, and enjoy the proper goodbye he'd thought the track would never get as the goodbye boiled through the streets of Portland, exuberant in its liberty, exultant in its clumsy, quicksilver passion. He was going to enjoy the rest of his life. Just as he knew that Amanda would enjoy the rest of hers. Just as he knew the slugs, those magnificent, majestic beasts, would enjoy this, their last few hours of mad abandon. No matter how this glorious chaos ended, it beat the hell out of getting put out to stud in a gray production farm or having your head smashed in a slaughterhouse because you weren't fast enough or strong enough.

Ace strolled as the slugs sang. After a few steps, he started singing himself.

###

About the Author

Portland author John Sunseri has had about sixty short stories published over the last fifteen years in various magazines and anthologies, and he's co-edited a couple of anthologies for Permuted Press. He has an upcoming story in *Electric Spec.*

*****~~~~~*****

The Wraith's Child

by Philip John Schweitzer

Even though her husband had grown large enough to calve off his own children, and even though he (like most of those born monsters, rather than made) disliked children, Mary didn't complain that she, herself, was barren. Even though, for as long as she could remember, the thing she'd wanted most was to bear a child, and even though her infertility had not changed in death, she wouldn't moan about what was not possible. Instead, she worked diligently to make the best of what was.

Every morning, she rose before the sunrise to sing the day into life. At noon, when her husband went out to collect a human for lunch (though she was a monster, herself, she was still too much a human to go for it), she mixed ash with falcon's tears to make their drinks. And, at dusk, before she sang the sun down again (Mary only required the elixir for sustenance), she spread what remained of that elixir upon the trees and the stream because it was a panacea (for the living) against heartache. If she could not cure heartache in herself, she would at least cure it where she could.

In these ways, she attempted to combat the selfishness of her longing with the selflessness of her actions.

Mary had been so hopeful about forgetting children when she died, but then she'd gone and gotten herself eaten by the monster who'd be her husband. And, when a monster eats someone, there's always the chance they'll come back as a wraith, bound to their devourer, rather than stay dead. Which is what happened to Mary.

She'd been in thrall to a vast and crushing hopelessness for some time before this thought occurred to her: Nothing will ever be perfect, but that doesn't mean some things can't be good, nonetheless.

Her husband, for one, was good, both to Mary and in the general sense. No, he wouldn't talk openly about a lot of things (like the calving, or why he planned to leave all his children alone in the forest), but her husband was literally composed of rock, so the occasional silences suited him.

Her husband's name was Barry, and he was, for all that he avoided certain conversations, a generally light-hearted sort of monster, who would announce the two of them at parties by shouting, "Everyone had better watch their steps, if they want to escape the dire clutches of Mary and Barry, the Scary Monsters!"

He was always making up little rhymes like that. And Mary loved him all the more for it, even if the rhymes were sometimes dishonest.

Because, Barry didn't look scary at all. What he looked like was a pile of rocks shaped to resemble an ape.

When he walked around their home, which was a ruinous old castle with parapets and arrow-slits and dungeons and not a single piece of roofing left anywhere on it—and which the wraith in Mary found desperately appealing)—the stones would come dislodged where he brushed against them. They would attach themselves to his feet, hands, and knees, and he would look like a large, warty child until his body subsumed them. This, he assured Mary, happened to everyone in his family. He claimed to know this, despite his never having met a

36

single sibling, nor either of his parents. This was also, he assured Mary, common in his family.

Mary, though, was rightfully scary. She bore all the marks of her violent death upon her, including torn flesh, dismembered bowels, and a general funk which tickled the nose.

Barry told her that she was the most beautiful creature he'd ever laid eyes on. She'd often catch him glancing sideways at her when he thought she wasn't looking, or would feel his gaze linger on the crooked doorways she'd walked through, as though they were portals to a more perfect place.

These things melted her heart.

They melted her heart so much that, when he told her it was time for him to calve off his children in the forest, as his father had done to him so long ago, she simply gave him a kiss, told him how much he meant to her, and sent him off into the thick-pressed trees which surrounded their castle.

Barry had never said how long he might be gone. At first, Mary did not worry.

She woke up in the mornings and drank water from the stream so that her voice would be crisp and clear for the sun. By lunch, she was in the forest, searching out falcon's tears and making two or three times more elixir than previously. In the afternoons, she glided up to the stream's source and poured all the elixir in, so that the woods around her castle fairly laughed with delight. And, at night, she not only sang the sun down into the trees in the world's most sorrowful alto, but also sang the stars up into the sky. She did these things with great focus and resolve, and, in this way, she distracted herself from Barry's absence.

After the first week, however, Mary found herself faltering in her melodies, missing the knack in her elixirs, and falling into sleep before the sun had even set.

Again and again, her mind returned to the children Barry could bring them, but which he certainly wouldn't. Little differences like these had often reminded Mary that they were, after all, from different worlds.

She'd always been accepting of his differences, just as he had been of hers.

But, acceptance is not the same as joy, and as Mary slept, she dreamt that she was a queen in her castle, a queen who could have whatever it was that her heart desired. She had children and she had her husband and she was happy without needing to even try.

When she woke from the dream, the easy happiness was reduced again to acceptance.

And this acceptance felt coarse, because Mary and Barry had always been more different than other couples.

The point was this: Neither Mary nor Barry was perfect for the other. It was only after growing to understand one another's wants and needs that they fit together so well.

Perhaps this was why Mary felt betrayed when Barry didn't offer to bring even one of his children back. It might have been foreign of him to do so, but he had adapted for her in stranger ways before.

In spite of her misgivings, she still staunchly refused to feel morose about it. Mary was a wraith of action, not of complaints. She looked at herself in the mirror and said to her reflection, "Now, Mary, feeling sorry never helped. Besides, you don't know what he plans; maybe he'll have known what you wanted after all, and will surprise you!"

But Mary knew that Barry would not surprise her. She knew this because he was like a child himself, when preparing gifts for others. He would giggle and laugh and rocks would collect on his body even more so than usual. Mary could always tell he was planning something when their castle developed great furrows in the floor, or grew windows in places none had been before. All through the days leading to his departure, Barry had barely smiled at all, and the stones had remained in their places.

The fretfulness in Mary grew, and her dreams did not stop, and the sun, without her voice to bring it up, rose heavily into the sky. The trees cried out from heartache.

Without her selflessness to shield her heart's sole desire, her want of a child wailed and struck at her mind's defenses, until they broke. She dwelled on the desire as never before and was made miserable by it. Children of all varieties strode past her mind's eye, human children with large eyes and thick fingers, and at the sight of these things, the wraith in Mary whispered to the human in her a grisly solution to her problem.

She could create a wraith (now that she was a form of monster, herself), in just the same way that she'd been made one. She could take a child, eat it, and perhaps it would rise up as a wraith for her.

Though the thing wasn't assured—such things never were—it was possible.

Mary knew in her heart what it was she considered, and the thought upset her human tendencies. But years of infertility had made her adept at fighting her heart, and so she decided to rest on her decision and see how it looked in the daylight.

By noon of the day following, she felt that the world itself validated her plan of action.

What happened to give her this impression was that the fire monsters arrived at her castle. They came every year, though Barry had always been the one to keep track of it. Without Barry, she could never remember when they were due.

The fire monsters were very much unlike both Barry and herself. They were tall. They were covered in red fur. They had cloven hooves. They had short, curling horns on their heads. They breathed, as one might expect, fire.

Every year, they came through to say hello to Barry (with whom one of them had been raised, after his own initial abandonment) before going off and razing a village or two in celebration of some holiday Mary could never remember.

There were always some corpses left, after they'd had their fun, and the whole affair gave rise to not a few wraiths. If the fire monsters left a young one, Mary thought she could perhaps help the process along.

Mary couldn't recall the name of the monster with whom Barry had been raised, as the fire monsters only ever came once a year, and Barry rarely spoke openly about his childhood, and she felt naked without this knowledge. But, if the monster was perturbed, then she gave no sign to Mary.

What she did give to Mary was a very large, and wholly warmhearted embrace, as well as the news that she and her kind had settled their celebrations on a small town nearby, that the town was very poor, and that it would burn easily.

She said, "Would you like to join us?"

What Mary gave the monster in return was a warm place to have a meal, a perfectly gloomy place to sleep, and the explanation (for she understood, from Barry's approach to the calving, that monsters couldn't fathom the drive for a child), "Barry is off calving now, and I expect him back soon." Though her mouth salivated at the idea of the feasting, she replied, "I was thinking of preparing a surprise for him. He loves roast children, but I'm no great hunter. I was wondering if you might leave one or two for me to bring him?"

What self-respecting monster could refuse such an earnest request?

So, the monster and her kind remained for a meal, a pleasantly gloomy sleep, and left with the morning sun warming their backs, although, the sun was not quite so warm as it would otherwise have been, had Mary sung it up in her usual style.

Mary waited another full day after they'd departed before heading out herself, and it's another testament to how inhuman she'd become that the sight of a hundred or more corpses with signs of burns and hungry teeth upon them made her dry, ghostly mouth water in anticipation.

She was surprised when she found six tiny, blackened corpses in the midst of the destruction. Mary had not expected so kind a gesture, even if the fire monsters were family, of a sort.

She took the infants into her arms, and brought them home. They were so light that, when she lay them upon the kitchen table, she wasn't the least tired.

A part of herself thought that they looked like such poor little things, lying there all blackened and fried. Another part leapt for joy at the prospect they brought. A third lusted after the taste of their flesh in her mouth. This was not helped by the fact that she'd lost her knack with the elixirs.

Mary ate the first of the children before going to sleep that night, and though no infant wraith presented itself to her, she did not worry.

In the morning, when she rose to the sunlight, a warm, pleasant wind crawled through the stone parapets, and the stream babbled, but these were the only childish things to be found. Mary remained unperturbed.

She walked to the table with the fixed persistence of a woman who knows her business. Five of the six children remained piled in a heap, and the bones of the sixth were arranged decoratively beside it. She wanted her child to enter the world seeing beauty, and bones are among the most beautiful things to a wraith.

Mary ate the second child with more purpose, as though purpose were a thing assured to change her outcome. It did not.

41

Noon came, and she ate a third, though still to no avail. The sun hung low in the sky when she sat down to eat the fourth.

In the morning, a vague sense of dread settled itself upon her shoulders.

After she'd had the fifth, she felt the creeping uncertainty of so few days prior set itself once more upon her.

Barry had been gone too long by then, and although Mary was aware that she knew little about calving, she was keenly aware that (in humans, at least) a week-long absence for birth was a frightening span.

Was calving a dangerous process? Barry had not given her cause to think so, though he was always loathe to make her nervous. He'd not smiled, nor joked, half as much as he usually did, even those times when he wasn't planning a grand surprise for her. In fact, he'd not smiled at all in the days leading up to his departure.

Mary sat and worried for Barry and told herself she was being foolish and berated herself for having focused so much on the children she didn't have, rather than on the husband she did.

That evening, she went out into the forest in order to look for him. She called his name with all her breath, but received no response from the close-pressed trees.

Distress grew in the pit of her stomach and pressed against her windpipe. Night dropped like a stone, and a dim light presented itself some distance before her. A voice called out her name.

"Mary," it cried, "Mary, I hear you. Where are you?"

It was the voice of the fire monster, Barry's adoptive sister.

"Mary," the monster said, "Are you all right? Come here, come here. It's so dark out, and you have no light."

"It's Barry," Mary said, feeling the rush of distress wash itself over her. "He's not coming back."

"Shhhh. Shh. Calm down now, Mary. Calving takes time. He'll be fine. Come on. Let's get you home."

...

In the morning Mary woke to the monster and her kind dining on the last of her children. The child lay dismembered on the table, but if the monsters were enjoying their meal, then they gave no sign. Their faces were dark, and their mouths wore frowns, and when Barry's sister caught sight of Mary, she rose.

"You said Barry wasn't here," the monster said, "And if Barry isn't here, then why are all the children we left for him eaten? I do not like being lied to."

Mary stared at the monster, and her distress pressed once more against her windpipe, and she told the monster everything. She told her how much she wanted a child, and how Barry had never offered, and how she had focused so much on the tiny wraith, and that this left no room for Barry.

The monster listened to Mary, and embraced her when she was finished.

"Mary," she said, "Barry will be fine. It takes time."

The monster picked something up off of the table and continued, "Here is the child's heart. We always save them for last. Though, if you'd been honest with us from the beginning, you'd still have the rest of the infants. Well, who knows. . . maybe it will bring you luck."

Mary's "Thank you," was a quiet response.

The monster turned to view her brethren and said to Mary, "We can't stay much longer, there are remembrances to be had. But, I'll come back in two weeks to check up on you and Barry. I'll even bring a few children, so that you, Barry, and I can have a feast."

Shortly after, the troupe stomped out of Mary's castle, weaving a trail of embers through the trees.

43

Mary did not eat the heart. Instead, she held onto it and squeezed it rhythmically in her fist, as though doing so would start it beating again.

…

Again Mary sat, that afternoon, on the parapets, squeezing the child's little heart in her hand, when she saw a small rock (only slightly larger than the child's heart) roll up to the foot of the castle.

Had Barry sent a child to her, after all?

She went down in order to greet it, her own dry heart fluttering in her ribcage, her smile burning white-hot on her face, the tiny infant's heart clutched tight in her hand.

"Mary," Barry said (how small he'd become!) as he rolled up to her feet. "It is so wonderful to see you again."

Mary bent down and lifted her husband to her breast and clutched him there, between the child's heart and her own. She sobbed once, quickly, and told herself she was foolish for it.

"What is that you have here, darling?" Barry said.

"Nothing," Mary said. "Nothing at all. Now, come inside, and I'll make us some of that elixir. You must be so tired."

###

About the Author

Philip John Schweitzer has been previously published in *Farrago's Wainscot* and *Strange Horizons.*

*****~~~~~*****

Besta Branco

by Tim Jeffreys

A horn blared, a group of dark-skinned children scattered laughing into the jungle, and a jeep rumbled up the dirt road into the village of Albapurus. The vehicle halted next to a row of shacks, and three white men, laden with rifles and equipment, jumped down from the rear. Seeing these men, two old women who'd been talking in the shade of a palm tree exclaimed under their breath, crossed themselves, and hurried on their way. They shouted at the children, who, curious, had come out of the jungle, telling them to get on home to their mothers. Something bad will happen today, they warned, worse than that day two months ago when spiders rained down out of the sky. The children were suitably startled.

The jeep circled around and tore off the way it had come, leaving the three white men looking about themselves in a swirl of dust. In the nearby shacks, doors were closed and blinds drawn. The residents of Albapurus had seen white men arrive in their village before. It happened more and more frequently. They came to pry and ask questions. They came with cameras strung around their necks and machines with which to make recordings. It was becoming obvious that Albapurus couldn't keep its secret from the wider world forever.

However, the three men who arrived that day on the back of a jeep had not come merely to snap a blurred photograph or record a distant rumble. The men were hunters, that much was clear at a glance. What the villagers couldn't have known, but might have guessed at, was that these men had made trophies—in their time—of the African Elephant, the Cape Buffalo, and the Rhinoceros. In India they had tracked and shot man-eating tigers. Far north of here they had brought down bears, moose, and bison. And they had come to the Brazilian jungle, to Albapurus, looking for a new challenge. They had come to hunt *Besta Branco*. The White Beast.

To look at, the three men—all tall and broad and muscular, all sporting white beards, all dressed in khakis and peaked caps—were indistinguishable from one another; but in reality they came from very different backgrounds. Bob Bernham, the leader of the group, was an ex-military man and had even been awarded the Purple Heart, but when the wars were over he'd never lost his lust for killing. John A. Jones was an American computer software billionaire, who hunted for sport and hung heads on the walls of his New York mansion. And finally there was Peter Blixen, an English explorer and academic, who viewed each fresh adventure, whether climbing mountains or stalking leopards in the African wilds, as a challenge not to his body but to his mind. Blixen was the only member of the group who could speak Portuguese.

Blixen carried with him a binder. The binder contained information which it had taken a team of investigators—paid by the hunters—six months to amass. When Blixen had first suggested the trip to Albapurus, Bernham had scoffed and said: "Then what? Bigfoot? The Loch Ness monster?" Yet the file of hard-won information returned to them by their investigators, though slim, nevertheless contained enough to convince all three that *Besta Branco* was real. It included reports of sightings and encounters dating back more than thirty years, film stills showing a pale body glimpsed through trees, photographs of giant footprints that had been looked over and assessed by experts, and drawings made by a traveller who claimed to have witnessed the beast whilst walking in the jungle. The only thing the team of investigators had not been able to discover was how one went about finding this monster. Now that the hunters had landed in Albapurus, they planned to discover this for themselves.

They took their time in gathering information. Starting at the Bar and Grill, Blixen began conversations with the locals, eventually bringing talk around to the local legend.

"Is it real?" he asked in the most casual way, stroking his beard, as if the purpose he and his companions had in coming here wasn't already clear to all. "Is there anyone in the village who has seen this *Besta Branco?* Is there anyone who knows where to find it?"

The people he spoke to shrugged and shook their heads. "We don't know what you're talking about," they answered. "We don't know anything about any White Beast." And they would try to laugh, but Peter— watching—saw something in their eyes, something like fear. He spent all day going about the village, even offering dollars and *real*, but no one would speak to him. At dusk the three white men set up camp amongst the first line of trees, and it was clear to the residents of Albapurus that their visitors were not the type to be easily deterred.

On the afternoon of their eighth day in the village, the three men were returning to the Bar and Grill when a man stopped them in the street. He was a thin, dark man in raggedy clothes. His face had a sunken look. There was no one about except a group of children of various ages playing with a ball nearby. The man tugged on Peter Blixen's sleeve, glanced around furtively, and spoke to him in hushed tones with his head lowered.

"It is said you look for the White Beast?"

A smile touched Blixen's lips. "Yes. Do you know where to find it?"

The man hesitated a moment. "My family. Very poor."

"I understand," Peter said, and took out his wallet. He counted bills into the man's hand until the man appeared satisfied.

"Where?"

"Deep in the jungle."

"Can you show us?"

"Not me, but. . . " The man turned to the group of children playing in the road. He gestured at a girl of perhaps nine or ten who had wispy black hair that floated above her head and wore a vest and orange shorts. "Her name is Duda. She is friend, they say, of the beast."

"*Friend?*"

"She goes into the jungle to visit it. Watch her, and wait. Soon she will go. You follow. You must tell no one who told you this."

Peter gave a snort, thinking that the man had played a joke on him, but something in the man's face, the quick dread, assured him otherwise.

At that moment there was shouting from further along the street. With a look of alarm the thin man glanced that way then turned on his heel and ran. A group of men had come out of the Bar and Grill. They chased the thin man, shouting and throwing rocks. The thin man was light on his feet and quickly vanished into the jungle. The men turned and walked back towards where the hunters were standing. They shook their heads. "*Louco!*" they shouted, pointing at their temples. "*Louco! No escutar! Louco!*"

"What're they saying?" Jones asked Blixen out of the corner of his mouth.

"They're saying he's crazy, and that we shouldn't listen to him," Blixen said, nodding to the local men. "Which makes me think we're on to something." He stepped back, allowing the locals to pass. They continued to shout and gesture all the way back to the Bar and Grill.

Blixen smiled at them, shrugging his shoulders and saying, "*Sim. Louco. Louco.*" This seemed to pacify them.

It was Bernham who followed Duda to find out where she lived. He and Jones set up a tree stand in the rim of the jungle and took turns watching the girl through binoculars. Bernham passed the time when he wasn't at the binoculars by using his hunting knife to strip a nearby tree of bark. Having exposed the creamy-white interior, he would stab at the tree with the blade, muttering: "White Beast. Here's what I think of your White Beast. Huh!" When Jones witnessed Duda leave her house alone one morning nine days later and walk to the line of trees with some clear intention, he radio-ed Blixen at once, and within half an hour the three men crept through the jungle in pursuit of the girl. They carried rifles and ropes and pockets full of ammunition.

Duda appeared to be at home in the jungle. She picked her way with ease, skipping about and singing to herself whilst the three men clawed leaves and branches from their path and wiped sweat from their faces. After about two hours walking, they arrived at an area of the forest populated mainly by long-leaved trees bearing reddish pods. Whilst the others watched, Blixen reached up and plucked one of the pods. Splitting the outer shell with his knife, he revealed the creamy yellow fruit inside.

"*Cupuacu,*" he told the others, offering the fruit for them to try. "They call it the taste of the Amazon."

"It tastes like nothing I've ever put in my mouth," Jones said, and he reached up to pluck another of the fruits for himself.

Hearing a voice from the jungle ahead of them, they realised they had lost sight of Duda and hurried on in pursuit. She had stopped in the centre of a clearing. She began shouting. "*Jacinto! Jacinto! Onde está? Onde está?*"

Bernham nudged Blixen. "What's she saying?"

49

Blixen went on watching the girl for a moment, puzzled. "She's calling to someone called Jacinto. It's a name. She's saying: where are you?"

"Who the hell is Jacinto?"

"Maybe this is some kind of trick," Jones said. "An ambush."

"No," Blixen said, his eyes still fixed on the girl. "I think that's what she calls it. That's her name for the beast."

The men fell silent. Duda went on calling, until all at once she stopped and threw out her hands, laughing, as if to embrace someone. Blixen gazed beyond her now, into the shadows of the trees. He thought he saw something moving there. He reached for the binoculars strung around his neck, when all at once a large white form stepped out into the clearing. Duda ran towards it with her arms spread, shouting again: "Jacinto! Jacinto!" Behind him, Blixen heard Bernham exclaim and say in a hiss: "What the Jesus is *that*?"

It was like some naked bat, but covered from head to foot in short white fur, and it was massive. If the three hunters had stood on each other's shoulders, they would not have been as tall as it was. It stood on two legs and had a pair of skinny arms under which where folded flaps that might have been wings. Its white head featured a huge pair of pinkish pupil-less eyes, and its mouth was like that of a shark, lipless and full of fearsome-looking teeth.

"Don't. Move. A muscle," Blixen whispered. His heart beat so hard and fast, partly from fear but also out of excitement, that he could feel his whole body rocking with the force of it. He was horrified by the sight of this thing, and by the sight of the child running towards it, dwarfed by its great grotesque form. *It's a monster*, he thought, his mouth hanging open, *some kind of monster. It will crush her and eat her. She should be running from it, running for her life. What is she doing? What the Christ is she. . . ?*

His thoughts went dead. He could only stare. It was the most truly bizarre spectacle he'd witnessed in his entire life, and would most likely ever witness, in a lifetime of adventuring. This towering monster ventured further into the clearing as the little girl sped towards it, then—to the utter shock of the three watching men—it ducked down and playfully nosed at her, knocking her off her feet. The men heard a ring of laughter from the clearing. Then, the girl—who now seemed tiny—and the monster ran together about the clearing. Now and then the creature lowered its fearsome head and knocked the girl over onto her back and Duda would laugh.

Some time passed before any of the three watching could make a sound that resembled words.

"She's. . . she's playing with it. That. . . that thing. She's *playing* with it."

"Unbelievable."

"Look," Blixen said, seeing the beast reaching into the trees. "It eats the *cupuacu* fruit."

They watched a while longer. Not one of them could have torn their eyes away if they'd wanted to. Time passed. The sun rose high over the heads of the trees; then it began to sink behind them. Jones was the first to come to his senses.

"Gentlemen," he said in a low tone, "what're we going to do?"

"We came here to hunt, didn't we?" Bernham said.

Blixen felt his heart pick up again. "Yes. Yes."

"What about the girl?" Jones said.

"We'll wait until she leaves. Then we'll go after it."

"Yes," Blixen said, smiling now and reaching for the rifle on his back. "Yes."

...

On the afternoon of the following day the three men emerged from the jungle. All three were drenched with sweat, and they laboured over ropes which they used to drag what looked like some great weight out from the dense green shelter of the trees. With shouts and exclamations, the residents of Albapurus began to gather. The old women crossed themselves. The children climbed trees to get a better view. At last a great, shocked sigh went up amongst the crowd as a massive white head was pulled from the jungle and onto the road. The big pink-tinted eyes glittered under the sun; the mouth full of teeth hung open with the long purple tongue lolling out. An angry tornado of flies hung in the air above the monster. The residents of Albapurus were horrified that this thing which until now had lived almost entirely in their imaginations had been dragged out into the sunlight; quite real, quite flesh, and clearly now quite, quite dead.

"We're back. We made it!" Jones said to his companions, with obvious relief. He looked dazed. He wiped the sweat from his brow with one forearm. "God, that thing is so heavy. And back there in the jungle, I thought it was the end. Just for a minute I thought this thing had got the best of us. And when it opened its mouth. Every time we put a bullet in it. That roar. I've never heard anything like it. It just. . . it stopped your heart. Awful."

"Now the world's going to see the pictures," Bernham said, grinning. "And we'll be on every magazine cover the world over. Our names will go down in history, John-boy, as the greatest hunters who ever lived. How'd you like that?"

Somewhere in the crowd, a child began screaming. A girl pushed her way through to the front. It was Duda. When she saw the body, her screaming turned hysterical. She threw herself on the body, bawling and shouting in a broken voice: "Jacinto! Jacinto!"

Bernham tried to pull Duda away as he wanted to get some pictures of his companions posing with the body before rot set in. But since Duda, in her hysteria, would not let go of the creature, he lifted her roughly by the arm and threw her down in the dirt. At this she shouted at him, and spat.

"Now how about...?"

Bernham turned to Blixen, who had the camera equipment, but the Englishman had gone pale and stood listening intently to Duda's ranting. There was a sudden commotion amongst the crowd. Woman and children screamed. People began running to and fro. They ran to their houses. Those who had cars loaded them with possessions. Other people ran down the dirt track, away from the village. Only a few minutes had passed before cars began speeding away down the road. The drivers shouted curses at the three hunters as they careered past them, whilst children cried, and dogs barked and chickens flapped and squawked in cages in the back seats of their cars.

Jones took Blixen, who stood still in some kind of trance, by the arm and turned him so that they looked at each other.

"What's going on? What did she say, that girl? What the hell did she say to cause all this hysteria?"

Blixen blinked, raising his eyes to meet those of the other man.

"She said that this is not *Besta Branco*."

"What? What the hell does that mean? If this isn't *Besta Branco,* what in God's name is it?"

"This is the one she calls Jacinto. The baby, she calls it. The child of *Besta Branco*. It's only the child."

"The child? You mean. . . ? There's more? More of them?"

"Two more at least. We killed the beast's infant child, that's all. Not the beast itself."

Jones, who had been listening, turned in shock and stared at the monstrous form lying dead in the road. "That *thing* is only an infant? Then the parents must be. . . a full grown one has to be. . . "

Bernham stepped forward and grabbed Blixen by the shoulders.

"And all this? All this panic? Why?"

Blixen swallowed. He seemed to struggle to focus his eyes on the other man. "She said that now the parents will come. She said the parents will be angry. She said that the parents will come and leave no house standing, and no man, woman, or child here alive." Blixen shot his head to the side. "*Listen,*" he said. "*Hear that?*"

Bernham turned his ear towards the trees. "What? What? I don't—"

He stopped talking when he saw Jones begin frantically pulling shotgun shells from his pocket and loading them into his gun.

About the Author

Tim Jeffreys has authored five collections of short stories, most recently *Another Shore*. His near-future sci-fi novella, *Voids,* co-written with Martin Greaves, was published by Omnium Gatherum in 2016. His short fiction has appeared in various international anthologies and magazines. He also edits and compiles the Dark Lane Anthologies, wherein he gets to publish talented writers from all over the world. In his own work he incorporates elements of horror, fantasy, absurdist humour, science fiction, and anything else he wants to toss into the pot to create his own brand of weird fiction. Tim is also a talented artist and gained a university honours degree in Graphic Arts and Design. Originally from the Manchester area, Tim now lives in Bristol with his partner and two young daughters. He has a day job with the Health Service and has no time for a social life.

*****~~~~~*****

How Not to Eat People

by Sarah Tchernev

[MUSIC]

Barry: Welcome to the podcast. I'm Barry.

Phil: This is Phil.

Barry: And you're listening to *Good Eating.*

Phil: [LAUGHS] We're on episode 37. I can't believe we've gotten that far. You'd think somebody would've shut us down by now. It's just that—

Barry: Of course.

Phil: The stuff we talk about is hard for some people to stomach. Which is funny, because we talk about stuff you put in your stomach. [LAUGHS]

Barry: That's a terrible joke, Phil. Our subject today is pizza. What to put on it, how to eat it, and how to get away with it.

Phil: Getting away with it is the hard part.

Barry: One thing I recommend is getting a steak and chopping it into inch-sized pieces, then spreading it around the crust really even. Then go down to your basement, and I hope you're keeping a dirty basement, and collect all the spiders you can find. Meat is great, but eating a living creature really keeps the cravings down.

Phil: Put honey on the pizza first so the spiders stick. Otherwise they'll crawl away, and nobody likes that.

Barry: Add some basil; that goes great with the raw meat. And eat it quick, before the spiders get loose,

55

but don't cook it first. It's the life in the food that keeps the cravings down. And if you don't keep the cravings down—

Phil: Humans start looking tasty.

Barry: You don't want to fall off the wagon. So follow our three simple tips for not eating humans: keep a dirty basement, eat raw meat, and never socialize while hungry. Humans are living, feeling beings with all the same rights to exist as you.

Phil: You know, humans are our friends, and we don't eat our friends.

Barry: If you have any good pizza recipes tweet them to @GoodEatingPodcast, and don't forget to visit our website at GoodEatingPodcast.com. We'll be back next week with tips on stews and soups.

[MUSIC]

[CREDITS]

...

[MUSIC]

Barry: It's Barry.

Phil: That's not Barry, I'm Barry.

Barry: [LAUGHS] That's Phil. He's a real clown, but we like him anyway.

Phil: Thank you.

Barry: And welcome to the podcast. It's *Good Eating*, episode 38. Today we're discussing tips on stews and soups. But first, Phil, I wanted to ask how your weekend went.

Phil: The usual, you know. House cleaning, chores, sharpening my fangs. Very, very normal. Nothing unusual happened. Nothing at all.

Barry: Huh, well. I saw a movie—

Phil: I ate a man.

Barry: I'm sorry?

How Not to Eat People

Phil: I was at the grocery store buying bouillon cubes for the show, and I saw this father standing in the cereal aisle. He was droning on about something and his son got bored and started looking around. Then the father snapped at him and started cussing. He called his son some nasty words, and the boy looked so defeated, you know, like this was normal for him. And it's hard to know what to do in a situation like that. If you tell the guy to stop it might make things worse. And you can't really call the cops because it isn't a dangerous situation. He isn't physically hurting the boy.

Barry: What did you do?

Phil: I followed them home in my car. It was night by then, so I waited outside their house. The father went outside for a smoke, so I walked up to the porch. He said "hello," I said "hey," and then I ate him.

Barry: Jesus.

Phil: Yep. Two gulps and he was gone. I hinged my jaw back into place and ran for my car. Then I drove home and waited inside with all the lights off. I was sure somebody was going to come for me, but, you know, nothing happened. How was your weekend? What movie did you see?

Barry: That's terrible. I can't believe you did that. After all the work we've done. All the workshops, the Twitter campaign, the t shirts. I mean, you haven't eaten a person in decades.

Phil: Something came over me. I don't know. Maybe I shouldn't be doing this podcast anymore. I feel terrible.

Barry: No, no, no. It's okay. Everybody falls off the wagon sometimes. The important thing is to get back on. That's the battle right there. Besides, the guy wasn't worth much.

Phil: Sure, I guess.

Barry: Although you still shouldn't have done it. But let's get back on topic. For a stew I recommend getting the water to room temperature and throwing in some flies—

Phil: I lied. A police officer came to my house the next day.

Barry: You said nobody caught you.

Phil: He didn't catch me. The officer asked me a few questions. He said a man went missing and my car was seen driving around the neighborhood. Apparently some old lady writes down the plate numbers of all the suspicious cars she sees. Crazy old lady. I can't believe the police take tips from somebody like that.

Barry: Well, what did he ask you?

Phil: If I'd been driving through the neighborhood. I told him, no, she had the wrong plate number. And he wanted to know what I'd been doing that night. I said I'd been boiling bouillon cubes for my cooking podcast. He laughed at that.

Barry: What a jerk.

Phil: I know. But he left eventually.

Barry: And you haven't heard back from him?

Phil: Nope.

Barry: If any other terrible things happened, you should tell me right now.

Phil: No, nothing. I took a nap. It was nice.

Barry: Huh, well, we should stop here then. This is *Good Eating*. Remember our three simple tips for not eating humans: Keep a dirty basement, eat raw meat, and never socialize while hungry.

Phil: People are people too.

Barry: And don't forget to follow us on Twitter.

[MUSIC]

[CREDITS]

...

[MUSIC]

Barry: This is *Good Eating*. I'm your host Barry—

Phil: The police officer came back.

Barry: You said nothing happened.

Phil: Nothing really happened. He asked more questions. And he brought some people with him, but they weren't wearing uniforms.

Barry: Those were detectives. Plainclothes detectives.

Phil: Right, well. They didn't say anything.

Barry: What did he ask you?

Phil: Not much. He showed me a picture of the guy I ate and asked if I knew him. I said no. Because I didn't know him. But he said the man's wife and son were worried about him. They had no idea where he was and they were sitting at home crying. That made me feel bad. So I told him I saw the guy at the grocery store.

Barry: I can't believe you said that. You're going to get us both found out.

Phil: It's okay. He only wanted me to do a lie detector test at the police station. Which I passed. With flying colors.

Barry: Oh, God.

Phil: And I mean that literally. The readout from the lie-detector was completely flat. I guess it doesn't work on our kind.

Barry: I did not know that.

Phil: And that's it.

Barry: You do realize it would be a disaster if the police found out what we are? You do comprehend that? We've been living among humans in secret for thousands of years. You're going to blow that with one murder.

Phil: But we don't eat people, just bugs and lots of raw meat.

Barry: They don't care. They'll lock us both in a lab. Then they'll hunt down all our friends and listeners. Besides, you ate someone. They're not going to trust you.

Phil: I can't stop talking to the police. It's the law.

Barry: Yeah, you can. Get a lawyer.

Phil: Oh.

Barry: I'm stopping the recording now. We need to talk.

Phil: That's fine. But, hey, listeners. If you know a special lawyer, and I mean a lawyer like us, tweet me. Maybe I should open a Kickstarter to cover the costs—

[MUSIC]

[CREDITS]

...

[MUSIC]

Barry: Hello. This used to be *Good Eating,* but now it's *Phil's Stupid Idiot Hour*.

Phil: That hurt.

Barry: As much as I want to stop this podcast, we're getting more downloads than ever. I guess people like listening to your stupidity. Anyway, we're raking in a lot of advertising money from those downloads, and we're going to need that money. You should tell them why, Phil.

Phil: It was late at night, like, really late. And I heard a knock. So I stopped sharpening my fangs and answered it. It was the police officer. But he wasn't wearing his uniform. He said he knew I killed the guy. I was so shocked I kind of nodded and said I'd actually eaten him. But that didn't surprise him.

Barry: And why didn't that surprise him?

Phil: Because he knows. He knows about our kind. That lie-detector test, he said that was how he figured it out. The machine only acts that way on people like us.

Barry: You forgot to mention the part where you told him my name.

Phil: Yeah. I didn't get to that part yet.

Barry: So I'm sitting at home and the police officer appears on my front porch. But he isn't wearing a uniform. Creepy guy too. He smiles this toothy grin and starts chatting with me about how nice my house is. Like I'm a realtor. Then he leans in close and tells me he knows my secret, and I better watch out. And like that, he walks off and disappears. Which is great. I really needed that in my life. So now we're trying to raise enough money to move away.

Phil: Yep. To the big city, or whatever.

Barry: But neither of us makes a lot of money.

Phil: Speak for yourself. I've got the graveyard shift at Arbys, and it's pretty sweet. They have a lot of bugs in there. Plus curly fries.

Barry: You're the worst. Anyway, I'm barely making my rent as it is. So, this is going to take a while—

Phil: We can eat the police officer.

Barry: Jesus. No. That's what started all this. The police will wonder what happened to their officer and come looking for us. Then, bam, we're in a lab at Guantanamo Bay.

Phil: I think he's doing this by himself. Police don't go out late at night without their uniforms.

Barry: Huh, good point.

Phil: So, yeah, let's eat him. I'll wear a trench coat and sunglasses. Nobody will recognize me. But you should wear something else, so people don't know we're together.

Barry: That's not a terrible plan. You should call the officer and say you have something to tell him, but you need to meet him in a back alley. Then we'll both jump out and eat him.

Phil: That'll work.

Barry: I can't believe I'm doing this. Okay, folks, I hope you enjoyed our messed up lives. If you want to send us money, visit our website at GoodEatingPodcast.com.

[MUSIC]
[CREDITS]

. . .

[MUSIC]

Barry: We're still here. We did not skip town. Although we probably should have.

Phil: It was great.

Barry: Yeah, no it wasn't.

Phil: Whatever. You enjoyed it.

Barry: So I'm standing in the alley behind the Chinese restaurant. The bad restaurant, not the good one downtown. Anyway, I hear voices, and it's Phil and the police officer coming down the alley. I don't know how Phil got him to agree to that.

Phil: I told him you were standing there waiting for him.

Barry: Really. That kind of blew the whole plan. The point was I was going to surprise him.

Phil: Oh, yeah.

Barry: You're so dumb I don't even know how you're still alive. Anyway, I jump out of the shadows and unhinge my jaw. My fangs are extended out really long. It's scary. I haven't scared any humans in a long time, and it was fun doing it again. But the police officer isn't scared at all. Not even a little.

Phil: The guy stands there with his arms folded. Really unimpressed. So I yell "surprise" but that makes him even more unimpressed.

Barry: The officer unhinges his own jaw and sticks out his fangs. He's one of us. He has been the whole time. That's how he knew Phil ate the guy. Anyway, we're standing there with our fangs hanging out, and it's really awkward.

Phil: The guy turns to me and says he found our podcast and he thinks it's stupid and we're a disgrace. Then he called me a stupid vegan. Which doesn't make sense because I eat meat.

Barry: He means human vegan.

Phil: Then he says he's going to kill us both because we're abominations. He takes out this gun. It's really big, like something the Terminator would carry. He aims it at me.

Barry: I yell to Phil that since the officer isn't human, it's okay to eat him.

Phil: So I take a bite.

Barry: And I take another bite. And there isn't anything left of him.

Phil: That was a filling meal.

Barry: He did not taste good. Listeners, if you're thinking about eating one of your own kind, don't bother. It isn't worth the effort.

Phil: I thought he was okay. Kinda dry.

Barry: I took his gun and threw it in the dumpster behind the restaurant, because I don't want the morning cook finding it. We went home after that.

Phil: Yep. Rode in the same car. Because Barry walked. He lives near the restaurant.

Barry: Now we're trying to save up enough money to move out of town. Like, to the other side of the country. So please keep donating to our Kickstarter. I know the money is supposed to go to Phil's lawyer, but we don't need that anymore. We're really close to our goal. Please keep the money coming.

Phil: This was a difficult experience, but I feel like I grew as a person.

Barry: How so?

Phil: I can see eating a human isn't worth it, even if they're a child abuser. It makes too much trouble. And even the worst human still has someone who loves them. It isn't fair to punish their family and friends. Killing creates an endless line of victims that can never be justified.

Barry: Wow. That's really articulate. But we killed one of our own kind. Didn't he deserve to live as much as any human?

Phil: Naw. That guy had it coming.

Barry: That's it for *Good Eating*. Hopefully you won't hear from us until we've moved to our new location. I'm not telling you where, because it's a secret. So don't forget to follow us on Twitter. Our name is @GoodEatingPodcast, and visit our website at GoodEatingPodcast.com.

Phil: Remember, the secret to not eating humans is keep a dirty basement, eat raw meat, and never socialize while hungry.

[MUSIC]

[CREDITS]

###

About the Author

Sarah Tchernev currently lives in Cincinnati, Ohio, where she is finishing her second novel.

*****~~~~~*****

To Riddle the Lake

by Lucy Harlow

—**riddle**, *v.1*

1. To separate (a person, quality, etc.) from another or others, as if with a riddle; to test or examine (a person); to extract or reveal (something) by separation or examination. *Obs.*

2.b. To pass (a substance) through a riddle; to separate with a riddle; to sift, sieve. . .

—*OED*

The age of water began with me, because I was the one who learned to riddle the lake. You might say that in doing so, I put out the primeval fire of this world's dry, bright, blazing dawn. I cannot say with certainty whether I believe one creature can bend time's rushing river and amend the wash of the ages, and yet I see that I have done it. The epochs turned on the axle of a riddled wing, and here in the deeps my metamorphosed soul is sated and complete.

In the cruel and glorious age of fire, I was a hunter. My dam hissed vicious incitements to violence at each day's birth, and I awoke with a rage that she sharpened with exquisite artistry. My anger she increased with pain and my hunger with deprivation: she held me down to test my power, and cut me all over with claw and tooth to make me brave. I cannot tell you whether the other dams were like this; I suspect not. I was unusually weak, and she, for her justification, required my survival.

You see, I was birthed an ugly, tattered thing, made of blood and feathers, bones and a radiant something between bones that was not quite tissue, but not quite spirit. Light passed through it, and my brothers and sisters couldn't stand to look in my direction. I was a grotesque reflection of them, appearing mysteriously flayed, yet impossibly intact. I was like, but dangerously unlike, and no one knew then that my horrifying body was no aberration, but the shape of the future they would never see.

For my difference, my dam tortured me into strength, and gave me the age's cruelty, though without its glory. After the pain, she cast me off the city's precipice to soar with my brothers and sisters on winding currents of heat and ash. The memory of her vicious whispers faded with the day's heat, but I slaughtered enough feathered fire-spirits to maintain my place in the pack. Their meat, when I was permitted to taste it, was all smoke and sulphur and molten blood.

But the day came when the very mountains ruptured, and bled out over our homes, scorching life out of dry land and driving us to the shores of the lake. Our only hope of meat was the thousand thousand scaly slimy slippery things that fed in the green depths of that deepwater stew. Down at the lapping threshold, my eyes took in the future, tear-steamed with dread.

My dam was relentless in her insistence that I join the hunt on the first day, but the water horrified me with a horror that I had not met before. I was afraid it would get between all the gaps in my being and freeze and force me apart, join me to the slimy waves, food of fishes, excrement of eels. That would be intolerable. I wanted to go back home and take my chances with the sputtering lava. I tried, but her power over me was still too strong.

To Riddle the Lake

My sire sired too many of the others to know which one I was, which is why I knew he would also require me to be dauntless on the shore. The correct occupation for the mutated weak is to absorb the damage and clear a path for the strong.

...

The first day. My dam sharpens my claws with her teeth. She tears at the quick, and I scream and scream and she does not flinch. She makes cuts in the radiant something between my bones to lure the lake beasts, and my blood considers the new ravines and trickles questioningly down them and onto the shore. It sizzles upon contact, hot and bright like the blood of the mountains that destroyed our homes.

I dip a feathered extremity into the water. Pain tears through me, fights blood back into vein, softens my arsenal, crumbles the sharp edges of my puissant claws. I cannot go on, and yet I must. The water closes in, penetrates my radiance until I am a limpid, gelatinous thing. I clutch my being like a cloak around me. This will not be borne.

Desperately I swipe at a passing creature, something serpentine and rot-soft. There is more of it than I thought there would be—I am not submerged, so I do not perceive it fully. But I draw it out and out, loop it around a clawed appendage, until eventually I find its limit, a shattered skull, a calcified beak and a dead eye. The creature stinks like carrion. With it, I limp back to shore.

I am bloated and slow as I drag my quarry to my dam. She unravels it, and the burning sun sucks out the ooze from along its length. The beak she severs for a trophy, but the desiccated remnant she casts aside. Not enough. Go deeper, tomorrow. Be submerged.

The sun and fire of day hold together my radiant being, but I metamorphose when night falls. My brothers and sisters lie on the shore, lumps of solid, dark flesh, but

I disperse. My consciousness is distributed to all my disparate parts, which rise into the atmosphere, the planet's undulating breath. I look down at her, spinning and tumbling and burning through vacuity, flailing in a crisis I cannot yet fathom. As she turns sunside I recoagulate and resume.

The second day, and I cringe from the shore as my brothers and sisters tread the waves. My dam seizes me in her claws as I shudder on the shore, and coats me all over with stinking grease. My slick feathers are flattened, thatching over my not-quite-flesh. I am afraid to stretch out, to disintegrate, so I wriggle back towards the lake, my extremities packed tightly about me. I insist that I cohere by day, though in dark and damp it seems impossible. I submerge.

Light behaves differently here; prey's signatures are confused, to me. I cannot remember where my claws are: I cannot feel the centre of myself, because the centre begins to seem everywhere. I concentrate on the hunt. Nothing of this world is pleasing to the taste, but I begin to recognise degrees of sensation. I move towards the zone of greatest intensity, and chase out something warm and plump. It is fast in the lake, but I herd it to shore, and it splutters and perishes on the beach.

Ah, blood, sweet, salt-bright; my dam's smile is a terrible thing. When she opens the carcass there is nothing for the burning sun to steal. It is devoured. She regards me with a twitching countenance. Why am I still alive?

Evening comes on the prongs of the moon. I metamorphose and return to the mountain. It bleeds and boils, still, and I wonder what will be born from the clotted remains when it ceases to flow. Somehow, I know that we will not return: there is no way back from the foot of the mountain, the shore of the lake. I send for myself along the sinews of my heart when morning comes.

My brothers and sisters are braver now, and they use my second-day strategy to chase ever greater monsters to shore. But I still cannot fathom the new hunting ground. I get trapped in the floating forests, spinning and tumbling and flailing in crisis. At the end of the third day I struggle to the shore, and my dam rages and rages at my empty claws. And there is, at last, a change in the pain she inflicts.

It is not preparation: it is not the artistry and rhetoric of pain. Gone is the articulacy of her sharpened claws and whispered cruelties, calculated to keep me alive and hungry. I have failed too much, and my survival is an insult. This is not an attack from which I will recover: now I am the hunted.

She holds me down and rips out the claws she sharpened two days ago. She slices deep gorges in the spaces between my bones. She plucks out one of my eyes. She wrenches a wing from the socket and casts it aside. The sun burns down, but my radiant matter protects my hesitant blood.

The others feast far from the oily rot of my corpse as the searing day darkens. In the fading light I force my remaining eye in the direction of my remaining wing, and wonder if my parts are already too widely dispersed for me to metamorphose. And then I notice something.

Like the light of the mountains, the lakewater has not recognised my not-flesh as an impediment. It has passed through the lattice of bone and feather and sinew, and has left behind countless tiny creeping wriggling things. There is no glory in grubs, but I tug wing to mouth and ingest them anyway. I begin to feel stronger.

One of my brothers has dragged my severed wing to the feast. I point the eye towards him. I feel no pain; only the hesitation of the blood.

They find the tiny creatures trapped in my riddled wing. They claw them out and devour them, and in the heat of fire and appetite they tug at their own wings for quarry. There is none: the lake creatures slid off their slick feathers and solid flesh. They fight and tear at each other, brother and sister devouring sister and brother, glutted with the forbidden taste of each other. Meanwhile, my sire takes my wing, drops it within the radius of my dam's glare, and slays her with a claw to the throat. My people cannot survive this night; all are lost for a severed wing riddled with holes.

I point my eye to the lake.

I drag the pulsing remnant of myself to the shore and wonder, for the first time, whether my brothers and sisters ever metamorphosed at the touch of night. I suspect not. All flesh and substance, they remained united to their bodies even as they were devoured. I was born different: sired, perhaps, by something worth slaying my dam for.

My line of sight skips over the ripples and to the imperceptible point where water meets sky. Why am I still alive?

I slide into the dark, tepid stew and, no longer resisting, give it my blood and breath; it gives back to me a strange alteration. My wing, wide and rare, metamorphoses, reaches far into the lake, trawling, seeking. I sense my deepwater cohabitants, the strangeness of their gear and tackle and trim. Moonlight filters down through the arching roof of water. I am alive.

...

That was the three-days' hunt which ended the world's first age, and I, dying, was at its heart. I felt no triumph in my survival, and mourned the countless deaths on the other side of the shoreline. I became the lake's strongest and strangest hunter, but I was alone as ever, even at the rising of the tides and the breeding of a new people, the regulation and affirmation of my mutation.

The world grew and changed, and I sank deeper and deeper. My lake converted to a great ocean, and time's rushing river broadened around me and could not touch me. I have tasted death, but it cannot reach me.

And so I am still here, beneath your continents and your oceans, and upon my riddled wing your world's age, too, will turn. I cannot say when, only that it will be soon. My pain, you see, has become great again, my hunger keen, my dam's whispered viciousness calling across the ages and goading me to hunt.

Soon for me is not the same as soon for you: may you live many happy lives before I rise! May your flesh be firm and your quarry calm, and your dams kind! But know that beneath it all, my wing trawls the bottom of the sea and feels the turning of the earth and tunes the music of the ages. I am waiting. I am alive.

About the Author

Lucy Harlow grew up in England and Hong Kong, and lives in Philadelphia, Pennsylvania. A graduate of the universities of St Andrews and York, she is currently a Ph.D. candidate at Princeton, writing a dissertation on medieval and early modern literature. She has published poetry in *Bracken Magazine* and has fiction forthcoming in *Aliterate.*

*****~~~~~*****

The Black Horse

by Philip Brian Hall

One hot late afternoon in June 1954, The Black Horse Inn on the Pickering road was packed. Mingling with local farmers on their way home from the cattle market, two charabancs full of day-trippers returning from the coast had disgorged their thirsty occupants.

Few indeed are the obstacles that can stand between a Yorkshireman and his ale. Pushing and shoving, a trio of brawny steelworkers forced their way through the sweating crowd to the polished, dark-oak bar where tall, ebony beer-pump handles promised speedy succor for the needy.

From their new vantage point the astonished men saw a fire incongruously burning in the bar's stone hearth. One of them irately demanded an explanation for the absurdity.

"Ar," the barman explained, "that there fire's burned nigh on two 'undred year. If'n it weren't kept constantly alight, sithee, Old Nick'd rise up an' carry all of us down to 'ell."

...

In the early years of King George III, a certain sporting squire of Kirkbymoorside named Tom Hargreaves came into possession of a splendid racehorse. Tom was a hard-drinking, hard-hunting landowner who

73

never saw a drink so large he couldn't down it in a single draft, nor a hedge so high he wouldn't set his horse at it for a bet. Many a time, by common consent, he should have broken his stupid neck, but he never did, and each success only emboldened him for yet further challenges. Folk began to say he enjoyed The Devil's own luck.

Many times his mare prevailed in point-to-point steeplechase matches with the best horses of North Yorkshire. She was never beaten, and eventually the local gentry and aristocracy grew tired of losing their animals to her insatiable owner. They declined to accept fresh challenges. In vain did Tom accuse all and sundry of cowardice and offer odds of two and three to one. Twice bitten, thrice shy, the celebrated horsemen of Bedale and Derwent were not to be fleeced any further.

Drinking far more than was good for him, in his frustration Tom became foul-tempered. He'd invested good silver in the mare, and he reckoned the world owed him a better reward. Sadly, all he could now hope for was that his horse's fame would not have spread far beyond the county boundary.

About a month after the mare's last race, a strange gentleman presented himself at the door of Kirkbymoorside Manor. Clad all in black, the olive-skinned stranger even had long, pigtailed black hair and a sharply pointed black mustache. Tom had never seen such coal-black eyes in the head of a living man.

"Good day to you Squire Hargreaves," the man said, greeting Tom with doffed hat and a sweeping bow. "My name is Zebub. I'm a jewel merchant from The East. I was told you were a keen sportsman, always on the lookout for a race."

Tom's eyes lit up with a green glint. A jewel merchant! Such men spent soft lives behind shop counters. "That I am, sir," he replied with a welcoming smile.

"Perhaps we could agree a time and place for our match and establish the stakes?" said Zebub.

"Why as to that, sir, the normal wager is one horse against the other, but perhaps as a traveler you find such an arrangement inconvenient and would prefer to offer an alternative?"

"How about these?" Zebub said, withdrawing from the pocket of his black frock-coat a black velvet bag, held tight at the top by a black drawstring. Opening it, he spilled into his palm a matched pair of brilliant-cut diamonds, each the size of a plover's egg.

"From the fabled mines of Ophir, these were once a gift to King Solomon from the Queen of Sheba," he declared grandly. "They eventually came into the hands of the Sultan of Stamboul, from whom I obtained them."

"Astonishing!" said Tom, his eyes widening with cupidity. "I fear, sir, I may struggle to find something of matching value."

"Oh, I assure you, squire, you possess something of equal value to me." Zebub leered knowingly. "But perhaps to increase the sport you will allow me to name your stake only after I've won the race?"

"You intrigue me, sir," said Tom, avarice leading him on to treacherous ground, "but since you won't win, I'll never know what I risked."

"In which case the loss will be mine, squire," said Zebub. "I propose a match to be raced at midnight. Since I'm not of your faith, I prefer not to race from one church steeple to another. I therefore suggest a race between the inn at the crossroads outside Kirkbymoorside and the inn at the crossroads outside Pickering. Come, squire, are we agreed?" He extended his hand.

Tom was so certain of victory he hesitated only a moment. "Please call me Tom. And your given name, sir?" he inquired. "If two gentlemen are to shake hands on a wager, it's only fitting they should know each other's given names."

Zebub smiled. "I fear mine are unpronounceable in your tongue," he said. "Why don't you just call me by my initials. Call me B. L."

Tom grasped the oriental's hand. "Then, B. L.," he said, "So be it. We shall meet at midnight."

As darkness fell and the evening wore on, Tom began to entertain sneaking doubts about what he'd gotten himself into. What if he should suffer an accident in the dark and be unseated? He'd trusted a stranger he didn't know from Adam with an unspecified stake that might end up costing him his home, his fortune, his lands—all for the sake of foolish pride. He resorted to his usual comfort in a bottle of Hollands.

By the time the clock struck eleven, Tom was sufficiently inebriated to have regarded any sudden emergence of hobgoblins from the hedgerow or pixies from the potting-shed as the merest commonplace. A gentleman could not withdraw from a wager without losing face and being handed the white feather, but what if he'd already been betrayed? What if mercenary footpads lurked at the crossroads ready to overpower him, steal his treasured horse, perhaps even murder him?

Tom swayed over to the sideboard, took out his twin, long-barreled pistols from their case, loaded and primed them, and inserted each into a holster for his groom to lace in front of his saddle.

Another half-bottle of gin later Tom heaved himself unsteadily aboard the mare and, muttering absent-mindedly in condemnation of his own folly, set off on a meandering ride along the short green road that led from his estate to the crossroads just outside the village of Kirkbymoorside.

The crisp night air steadied him only a little, but the full moon was bright, and at a walk he could see his way tolerably well, even if upon occasion he perceived two roads running in parallel between two identical avenues of old limes. Soon, however, one hand resting

76

nervously on a pistol, he drew rein outside the local hostelry, where only a single lantern burned over the door and all was dark and quiet within.

"Halloo!" he called softly. "Mr. Zebub, are you here?"

A clatter of hooves across the cobbles of the inn yard sent Tom's heart racing into palpitations. He was relieved when his challenger emerged into the light of the lantern, smiling broadly and mounted on a horse as black as his clothing.

The Arab stallion the eastern merchant rode was not large, no more than fifteen hands high, but he was strong. The beast's burnished coat gleamed like molten pitch in the light; his flowing mane cascaded down over a fine curving neck and short, handsome head with dark, flashing eyes. His chest was broad, his legs well set-on, his quarters bulging with sufficient muscle to carry him at great speed over any height of obstacle, and his tail was carried proudly tilted upwards at the dock.

"B. L.," the rider said as he approached. "We agreed, did we not, Tom? Two gentlemen should call each other by name?"

"We did, B. L. I'm very glad to see you. That's a fine animal you have there."

"We are well matched, Tom. And now, are we ready?"

"That we are, B. L. See us here together at the start. Now the winner's to be the first of us to draw rein within the stable yard of the inn this side of Pickering. Agreed?"

"Agreed."

"I shall count down from three. Three, two, one, go!"

As one the two riders set spurs to their horses' sides and galloped off. The black columns of tall trees on either side of the way, intersecting the eerie moonlight, flung deep shadows across the silver sliver of road.

Banshee cries of a startled barn owl screeched from the air above them, and from time to time bright eyes gleamed from the verge as nocturnal foxes or badgers took shelter from the onrushing steeds. The wind of their passage through the cold air made Tom's eyes water.

At first Tom's mare gained an easy lead, her long legs giving her a cruising speed considerably faster than the nimble but smaller Arab. Yet over the regular pounding of her hooves Tom always heard the faster cadence of the Arab's remorseless stride. He knew by repute that the stamina of a Barb was bottomless. Zebub's animal would never tire. Though his own mare had speed to burn, her endurance over such a long trip had never been tested.

What was the unspoken forfeit Zebub would demand should Tom lose the race? He hardly dared imagine the potentially devastating consequences if he lost his way, or if his mare stumbled, set hoof in a rabbit warren, or even cast a shoe. How greatly he regretted having drunk so much earlier in the evening.

Zebub? What kind of a heathen name was that anyway? What foreign pest-hole had the strange merchant come from? "Zebub" the hoof beats sang in his frost-pinched ears and troubled his sozzled brain. "B. L. Zebub. . . B. L. Zebub. . . Beelzebub!"

The shock of realization was almost sufficient to cause Tom to snatch up the reins. His eyes started from his head, certain now that malignant demons lurked behind every tree.

The Devil's own luck men used to say he had; well, now the Devil had come to have it back! He knew at once what forfeit the Sultan of Stamboul had redeemed with the costly diamonds. The very same forfeit would be claimed of Tom himself! How truly did The Good Book say it would profit a man nothing to gain the whole world at such a price.

The mare felt his sudden fear, communicated to her in that mysterious, wordless language that unites every horse and rider the world over. Uncertain what was to be feared, but knowing her rider sensed something amiss, she slackened her pace.

"On! On! On!" Tom screamed in panic, raking his spurs across her ribs and sending her leaping forward again at her best pace. It was a fatal mistake. In his terror he pushed the gallant mare too hard too soon, and long before they thundered through the little hamlet of Aislaby, barely two thirds of the way to Pickering, he felt her stride begin shortening and her breath becoming labored. The dread fingers of inexorable doom began to tighten their grip around Tom's heart as vainly he plied his crop upon his good mare's innocent hide.

And now, just as a man listening intently for a clock to chime will first notice the little inner whirs and clunks of the timepiece clearing its throat, Tom heard with a sense of dread the hoofbeats of the black stallion drawing ever closer behind him. Soon he was sure the Arab was right on his tail. Twisting in his saddle to look over his shoulder he unbalanced his own mare and slowed her yet further.

The sight was enough to freeze the blood of mortal man. The eyes of the demon steed blazed crimson and smoke poured from his distended nostrils as he breathed fire like a dragon, singeing the mare's tail. The pounding of his hooves struck showers of sparks from the unmetaled road as he devoured the ground with giant strides, his rider crouching low in the saddle.

Soon the black horse was alongside the faltering mare. Tom and The Devil rode stirrup to stirrup, neither yielding an inch of road to the other nor giving way on any bend. The two of them careered along like stampeding cattle from whom a pack of wolves has driven out any bovine thought but a desperate need for self-preservation.

But all Tom's effort was for naught.

"Now, Tom," Zebub called gleefully as the black stallion began to draw ahead. "I have you now. Your mare has shot her bolt!" A triumphant peal of demonic laughter echoed back from the bleak moorland hills to the north.

Tom could swear he saw horns on the stranger's head and hellfire burning behind the coal-black eyes. Beelzebub! Old Nick! Satan! Call him what you will, The Devil has me, and he won't let me go!

In vain Tom belabored the poor mare and dug his spurs into her sides. The honest creature had given her all and was running on exhausted memories of the fine talent she'd once possessed. Only her bravery and willpower even kept her upright. The black stallion drew inexorably away and had a ten-length lead by the time the dark shape of the inn at the Pickering crossroads loomed up out of the moonlit shadows of the road ahead.

In his desperation Tom knew he'd only one chance. The rider ahead was immortal, but maybe the horse was flesh and blood. Gripping the reins in his left hand, with the right Tom drew a pistol, cocked it, and, aiming at the black, flying shape in front of him, pulled the trigger.

When sober, Tom might have hit such a mark from the back of a galloping horse one time in ten. When drunk he'd no right to hit it at all, but whether he did or no, the onrushing black beast planted a front foot as only a flying horse can and jinked violently away to the right, sending his unseated rider flying headlong over his left shoulder and into the cobbled yard, where he landed heavily and lay still. Never checking his stride, the black horse galloped on over the crossroads, down the road into Pickering and away into the night.

When Tom drew rein in the inn yard, he dismounted, and, wobbling on legs debilitated not only by drink but also by fear and exhaustion, he tentatively approached his fallen opponent. Zebub lay motionless.

"My race, I think, sir," Tom said quietly. "You never drew rein. First to draw rein in the inn yard, we agreed, not first to dash out his brains on a stone!"

In truth a dark pool was already forming beneath the inert figure's head.

Tom heard a commotion behind him as the innkeeper flung open the door and emerged from the hostelry's newly lit threshold with a blunderbuss in his hand.

"Who's there? No honest man's abroad at such an hour. Be off about your business, or I'll shoot!"

In this moment of urgent need, Tom at last recovered a vestige of his fine wits. Kneeling beside the body, he extracted the black bag from Zebub's pocket and checked that the diamonds remained within. Rising again, he turned to the landlord.

"No one's here, innkeeper. You've seen nothing. Two villains rode by here at a furious pace. One may have fired a pistol. You heard a disturbance but you saw nothing, do you understand?"

"There looks to be a dead body here to testify against such a tale, squire," said the innkeeper, recognizing Tom's voice and approaching.

"But if the body is never found," Tom whispered savagely, "it can give no evidence. And if it gives no evidence, then you will find yourself amply rewarded for your trouble."

He showed the man the two diamonds. "I want nothing to remind me of this accursed foreign creature," Tom said, indicating the body. "He's already taught me a lesson more valuable than any shiny baubles. These are yours if you'll help me bury him in a place no-one will ever think to look."

The innkeeper looked at the diamonds glinting in the moonlight as they lay in Tom's palm. He looked at Tom. He looked back at the diamonds. Then he took a deep breath and reached a decision.

"Let's us carry him inside, squire," he said. "I know the very place."

...

"What?" said the furnaceman "They buried 'im under t' fireplace there? Tha's 'avin me on."

"Nay," the barman declared. "There's nob'dy as'd think to search under a lit fire, would they?"

"But was it really the Devil or just a traveling jewel merchant?" the furnaceman demanded.

"'Oo knows? Nob'dy's likely to risk tryin' ter find out, eh?"

"And what about t' 'orse," the furnaceman persisted. "The Devil's black 'orse—what became of it?"

"Never seen again," the barman responded, tapping the side of his nose and giving the furnaceman a wink. "Though there are folk 'ereabouts as say they've 'eard it, now and again, on a crisp night of a full moon like, still gallopin' along t' Pickering road a-lookin' fer its master."

"Well," the furnace-man exhaled slowly. "I've 'eard some tall tales, but this 'un takes all the beating. Aye, an' speakin' of beatin', tha'd best 'urry up an' pull us some ale. I've stood 'ere too long. If I don't get a drink outside to my missus in t' next five minutes there *will* be t' Devil ter pay!"

About the Author

Yorkshireman Philip Brian Hall is a graduate of Oxford University. A former diplomat and teacher, at one time or another he's stood for parliament, sung solos in amateur operettas, rowed at Henley Royal Regatta, completed a 40-mile cross-country walk in under 12 hours, and ridden in over one hundred steeplechase horse races. He lives on a very small farm in Scotland.

In addition to Third Flatiron's *It's Come to Our Attention* anthology, Philip's had short stories published in the USA, Canada, and the UK. His novel, *The Prophets of Baal,* is available as an e-book and in paperback.

He blogs at sliabhmannan.blogspot.co.uk.

*****~~~~~*****

Glass

by Jean Graham

A grimy window suits me fine.

A good coat of grime lets in less light while I sit my lengthy vigil on the peeling, also-grimy windowsill. Taking roach shape suits me, too. Roach shapes are perfect for abandoned houses. Thousands of our natural cousins already reside in this one.

Four weeks we've waited. Waited for George Mollet to come back to the house where he once lived—and killed. When he returns, and he will, his dissolute soul is going to be ours to devour.

We are George Mollet's death.

"I'm bored, Shard. Bored!" That's Servia, whose splendid hissing cockroach shape has crawled up the wall to join me on my sill, long antennae twitching in vibration with her words. "I'm so damned bored I could just puke!"

"By all means do," I tell her. "A little roach puke could only improve the place."

In truth, the house is already a cornucopia of tasty filth. Dust, mold, drug needles, both rat and human feces, and my personal favorite, rotted scraps of squatters' fast food dinners. Delectable!

Servia, however, is unimpressed with my suggestion. *"Pffffft!"* she hisses, antennae twitching still more furiously. "When is this asssssshole sssshowing up, anyway? I'm sssick of waiting. It's just sssssso boring!"

"Patience, sweet Servia, patience," I say, purposely mocking her sibilance. "The wrecking crew shows up bright and early tomorrow morning to knock down the house. That means he's got to do the deed tonight."

"Yesssss!" Servia executes a gleeful triple-pivot cockroach dance. "He hass to move poor Dead Darla, doesn't he? Ssso they won't find her when the walls come down."

"That he does." What's left of George's girlfriend Darla has for ten years been languishing in a 50-gallon oil drum walled up in the basement. Safely hidden forever. Or so he'd thought. "Shouldn't be long now. Not long at all."

My words prove prescient when Slash makes a typically showy appearance, a plump black roach dropping down from the ceiling. He lands between us, upside down, with a *plop,* rights himself, and says, "Truck just pulled into the alley behind the house. Stopped right behind the gate. Has to be our boy."

Our rush to the back door agitates the cousins, who skitter across the moldy carpet in a roachy brown wave, rustling like dry leaves in a breeze.

George is already jimmying the lock when we get to the kitchen. Not that it's a hard lock to jimmy. It's been broken and repaired a dozen times since the city condemned the place. But it takes him awhile, just the same.

"Doesn't he still own the house?" Slash wants to know. "Why doesn't he just use his key?"

"City must have changed all the locks," I reply. "Technically, they own it now."

Finally, the door is shoved inward, scraping over broken tile and garbage, and our mark steps inside. His booted feet crunch on the debris as he goes briefly out again and comes back carrying an enormous duffel bag that clanks and rattles as he moves. We already know what's in it. He'll need tools, won't he, to break down the wall and free Dead Darla's oil drum.

The bag *crumps* onto the counter top, so close to our hiding place behind the corroded faucet that we feel the air current it generates. The zipper grates open. George tosses in the screwdriver he used to break the lock, and extracts a femur-sized flashlight. When he switches it on, more dry leaves rustle across the floor, a legion of cousins scattering to escape the light. George swears and slams a foot down on several of them. We delight for a fleeting moment in odeur de squashed roach entrails. But then George snatches up the duffel and tromps across the kitchen to the cellar door.

It's locked, but he doesn't bother with the screwdriver this time. One brute force kick aimed just above the knob, and the door splinters into complete submission. With much thumping and scraping, George, duffel, and bobbing flashlight beam are all swallowed up by the newly made opening.

We waste no time in following him down the rough-hewn wooden stairs. We take up positions on a dilapidated metal shelf and watch George start rummaging anew in the bag. He produces a battery-powered camping lantern, flicks the switch, and the large room is immediately flooded with bright LED light, prompting us to retreat behind a rusty coffee can that occupies our shelf.

We know about this space, though we've never seen it until now. The damp, mold-puissant concrete walls are lined with dust-covered metal shelving, much of it still littered with broken remnants of the ceramics Darla once made here. They're still here, we know, because no one has lived in the house since George moved out to shack up with a new girl two cities away. He'd kept up with the mortgage and the property taxes. He'd just never counted on the city condemning the place.

We watch him prop the lantern on one of the shelves, pack his flashlight away, and schlep the duffel over to the back wall—the only one that isn't concrete – under the stairs. He passes Darla's kiln on the way, casting his shadow on the double-paned window in its tall steel door.

"All right, bitch," he says to the wall, and pulls a pick axe from the bag on the floor. "Time to roll out."

The drywall succumbs to his blows in minutes. When the chalky dust cloud clears, we can see Darla's barrel jammed between a bare earth embankment and the wooden four-by-fours supporting the foundation. We wait while he strains and grunts to free it and finally resorts to using the flat end of the pickaxe as a pry bar.

Dislodged at last, the oil drum rolls downhill and snags with a resounding *thud* on the broken drywall's edge.

More grunting now as George muscles it into position and drags it, steel scraping on concrete, out onto the floor. When he upends it, we hear the rattle of what can only be bones.

Darla is still in residence.

He's in the process of using the axe to pry open the lid when we venture out into the light and crawl down the shelf strut to inch across the floor toward him.

George doesn't notice.

The barrel's lid comes free with a protesting *skreek,* and at once the odor of charred flesh and bone floats free. We stop to relish that for just a moment, drawing Darla's essence into ourselves. Servia takes the lead then, morphing into human shape—Darla's shape—as she moves.

"Hello, George."

The barrel lid slips from George's fingers and crashes to the floor with a deafening *clang.* He stumbles back against the broken drywall and begins to stammer. "What. . . what the. . . ?"

Servia closes in on him, in all likelihood startling him all the more for the fact that in human guise, she never bothers with clothing.

"What's the matter, Georgie?" she coos. "Surprised to see me?"

"You're not. . . you can't. . . you're. . . you're. . . "

"Dead? Yes, I am. Thanks to you. Ten years I've waited in that barrel. No friends, no family, no one to even notice I was gone. But I knew you'd come back for me eventually."

She's very close to him now, and with a bellowed obscenity, George grabs her by the throat and tries to choke her. Servia laughs at him and presses on until he's pinned, struggling, against the wall, where she forces his head to one side and uses her sharpened fingernails to open a jugular vein. First feeding.

Slash and I have scurried up the oil drum's side and balanced on the rim to peer in at the real Darla's mortal remains. Nothing left but bone fragments and ashes.

A kiln makes an excellent crematorium.

The enticing smell of blood draws our attention away, though, and we rush to join Servia's feast, taking rat shape as we go. There's one trouser leg apiece for us to run up, and a rich supply of veins above George's sweaty socks. He writhes and swears at us, but he can't break Servia's hold on him.

We feed until each of us is satisfied. The liquid bounty, though, is only the appetizer.

Our rat shapes crawl out and up the outside of George's khaki pants, across his chalk-dusty sweatshirt and onto Servia's outstretched arms. We settle on each of her lovely bare shoulders, the better to address George directly, and Servia frees one hand from his chest in order to stroke both of us in turn.

"These are my *very* old friends," she informs him with a smile. "Slash. . . " Another stroke. ". . . and Shard."

Her nails skritch behind my small round ears. If rats could purr. . .

"We've been waiting for you, George," I say, and he jerks under Servia's grip, staring at me wide-eyed. It's not every day, I suppose, that you meet a conversational rat.

"Four weeks," Slash adds, making George's eyes dart in his direction. "Four lonnnng weeks."

"We were getting bored," Servia says.

"And hungry." I bare my sharp front incisors at him, a rat's toothy grin.

George tries to shrink into the wall. "What. . . " he stutters, ". . . w-what *are* you?"

Slash, with brutal honesty, answers, "Your death."

"Some. . . " Servia's long, slender fingers caress his beard-stubbled cheek. ". . . call us harvesters. Or soul reapers."

With an enraged roar, George shoves us backward and bolts in desperation for the stairs. He stumbles, but wouldn't have made it anyway. Two large brown rats, eyes glowing red, are there ahead of him. He staggers away from us and slams against the wall beside the kiln, knocking over the baking racks he removed ten years ago to make room for strangled Darla's corpse. Metal crashing onto concrete reverberates for several seconds, during which Servia melts out of Darla's nude body into rat shape as well. The three of us pause for a while, sitting together on the stairs and staring down our terrified prey. We're rat-shaped cats with a mouse.

The mouse is shivering now, from blood loss or fear or both.

"Your soul is ours, George," Slash says. "And we'll savor every ounce of it before we send it on to its reward. You have no idea how delicious a corrupt soul can be."

George has one last surprise in him, though. He launches a new string of obscenities at us, turns and

90

wrenches open the kiln's heavy door. He all but falls inside, and drags the door shut behind him with a wall-shaking *thud.*

"Well," says Servia. "That was unique."

"A pity the power's not on," Slash laments. "We could have crisped him up good and let what was left of him 'drop in' on Darla over there."

Truth to tell, I'm a little sorry about that myself. "Ah, well," I say. "There are, fortunately, other ways." And I lead a rat march to the kiln door, where we climb just high enough to peer in at George.

He's doing his damnedest to climb the oven walls, presumably to reach the vent pipe. But his weakened state and the lack of an adequate foothold are defeating him. He finally leans, exhausted, against the door and twists to glare smugly back at us.

"You can't get in, you bastards. I've jammed the lock from the inside." He mouths the words, assuming we won't be able to hear him out here. He's wrong. On both counts.

We mount the kiln's glass window as a unit, and our forms begin to melt as we climb. Both panes of the glass melt easily beneath us. We merge with them, shaping ourselves into a molten canopy of just the right size, and then. . .

We ooze down over George's head.

He screams and claws at us, but nothing can dislodge us now.

"You can't shut us out." Servia's voice caresses him as we flow inside and begin to leech and feed upon the dank, dusky blotch that is George Muller's soul.

"We can become anything, George," Slash murmurs. "Anything at all."

And mine. . . Mine is the final whisper to a dying soul.

"Even glass."

91

About the Author

Jean Graham's fiction has appeared in the anthologies *Memento Mori, Misunderstood, Time of the Vampires,* and *Dying to Live*, as well as in *Mythic Magazine.* A member of both SFWA and HWA, she resides in San Diego, California, along with 5,000 books, six cats, and one husband.

*****~~~~~*****

Creatures

by Marc E. Fitch

It was an eerie and uncanny sound coming from such a creature, the sound of an infant crying. It paced behind the bars of its cage like a tiger at a zoo, all anger and pent up frustration. We stood there in the room, three men and one woman of science, the only four people working at the Tanzer Biological Research Facility, and stared. Its gaze kept landing on Dr. Knowles, and then it would grow calm and still and start emitting that sound. Even after watching it happen, hearing the sound echo from its throat, I was still tempted to turn and see if a newborn child had been secreted into the room. Dr. Knowles did her best to maintain composure, but as it stared at her with those eyes and mewled, she finally turned away and left the room. I followed.

"Are you okay?"

"I just. . . I just can't do it with that thing looking at me like that, making those sounds. I can't stand it anymore. It's obscene."

"A tiger or lion would be looking at you the same way—food."

"No," she said. "A lion or tiger would be looking at *all of us* like we were food. This thing just wants me, just wants the women. It's an abomination!"

"We need to find out more about it. Where it came from. How we never found it before."

"It has been two days already! We need to put it down, out of its misery. Then you can dissect the hell out of it and learn all you want, but that thing needs to die now!"

"We can't do that yet," I said.

She turned to me, nearly crying. "You don't understand! I go home—to Aiden—and when he cries. . . I can barely bring myself to pick him up. I can barely bring myself to walk up the stairs to comfort my own baby."

"You don't have to worry, Susan. It's here. It's never leaving."

"You think that's the only one? Don't be ridiculous. And it's not just that. It's the eyes, the mouth, the teeth. It's horrid, and it's all I see when Aiden cries. I have to send Jim up for him every night."

"I know. . . "

"No. You don't. I'm the only one in here, Matthew. The only woman, and it just keeps staring at me and reaching out at me."

We stopped talking for a moment. The infant noises had ceased, and the whole place was silent as a grave.

"When are you announcing this, Matthew?"

"Soon," I said.

"It better be," she said. "Or I'll go to the press myself. How many women, Matthew? How many?"

"You know there's no way to know. . . "

She turned and left. I followed and watched her Range Rover bounce over the broken concrete road that led from our outpost in the pine hills surrounding Clarence Notch—a small, picturesque town bordering the Pacific. I returned to the holding room, and the other men looked at me. I just shook my head. They seemed to understand. We all thought we did, at least. But this was different, and I think we knew it on some level.

94

"Are we putting this thing down, Matthew?" Eric Joiner said.

"Not yet. Keep filming it. Soon."

"It's enough to make you give up on science altogether."

"And what?" I said. "Return to belief in demons?"

"It is what it is."

...

I stayed through the night, watching it. I wasn't even working, just sitting in my chair and watching it move, watching how it breathed. At night it was alive. Its vibrating vocal chords echoing the sounds of crickets and tree frogs like any forest on any night of any year. On its hind legs it was over six feet tall and reared up when I approached the cage—almost like a bear. Its skin was a slick black, reptilian leather. In the darkness one could only see its eyes, and I stayed back, because it would occasionally reach its arms through the bars with those massive claws and try to grasp anything that came near. The claws, as best as I could figure, were probably for digging. A burrower, like a badger or wolverine, and then, of course, for hunting and killing. . . but only women. Only female human beings, as far as we could tell. And to hunt its prey it made that sound—so terrifying in its implications. The last victim (that we knew of) had been lured away from her campground by the sound. She wandered into the dark woods. She had been part of a hunting party that were a day's walk into a forested mountain range and in the night thought she heard the sound of a baby crying. They searched the woods for days afterward. Helicopters and rescue teams. They tracked the signal from her cell phone. They found an underground lair. They found it. And the bones.

I drifted off to sleep sometime in the middle of the night. I don't know how I was able to do so, but I felt oddly comfortable with it after a time. I sympathized with Susan. Maybe I couldn't understand it fully. But then, maybe her judgment was clouded by fear and disgust. I woke suddenly to the sound of the door slamming shut and footsteps that echoed across the empty laboratory floor just beyond the holding area. It was still dark, the darkest of times, just before the dawn. I got out of my chair and walked through the locked doorway and into the main area, expecting to see one of my colleagues starting the day early, but there was no one there. There was nothing but the quiet drone of the computers running in sleep mode, only *my* breath, only *my* footsteps, only the sound of *myself* closing the door. I turned and walked back into the holding area. It paced back and forth like a caged cat, then reared up on its hind legs and stared at me with those eyes that penetrated to my soul.

...

"What the hell are we going to call this thing?" Shenkstein said.

"Hell-beast doesn't work for you?"

"This is an entirely new species; we just can't put it down without documenting, cataloguing, finding out as much as we can. What sex is it? How many others are there?"

"And how are we supposed to do all those things *without* putting it down?"

"You don't just kill off a one-of-a-kind species."

We understood Shenkstein's sentiment. The creature was hypnotic in a way. Merely the idea that we were witnessing and in possession of an animal previously unknown in all of history was something that touched us all in a strange way. That it could stay hidden for so long despite the evidence it left behind—missing women, probably thousands—baffled the mind. But then maybe missing, the disappeared, dead, and long forgotten was such a part of our world that no one ever suspected something like this could be responsible. Instead we accepted it as a part of life and moved on.

But what was it? What phylla? What evolutionary line did it descend from? How would one even start to guess? We once again found ourselves just staring at the thing and it staring back at us. Then it began to pace on its four legs again and the sound of a baby crying emanated from somewhere in its deep throat. Susan walked through the door.

"That thing knows she's here before we do," I said.

Susan's eyes seemed wet from stress and anger. She said, "I've contacted the federal government, gentlemen. They will be here within a day."

"Why would you do that?" Joiner screamed. "They'll take over everything! We won't get within a mile of this animal again!"

"It's not an animal," she said. "It needs to be disposed of and any others hunted down and killed as well. This is not a creature that should be allowed to continue. If the government sits on their hands too long with it, I'll go straight to the media and let the women of the world know exactly what is going on. It will be on all of you, so I suggest you figure out what you're going to do and do it fast."

We all looked at each other.

"You should have talked to us first, Susan," I said.

"I did," she said.

"It's not a monster, Susan. It's an animal, just like any other animal."

The crying continued. It gained in intensity and depth. She put her hand over her mouth to stifle a choking cry. "If it was just an animal—just a predator—why does it single me out? That is not animal behavior! That is intent. It's like murder! Do you know they use the sound of infants crying as a form of torture?" she said. "When you kill it, I want to be here, I want to watch."

"I don't think we're being scientific about. . . "

She turned and walked out the security doors.

The phone in the office began to ring.

The caller ID said it was coming from Washington. None of us answered.

"We have to document everything. This will be the biggest discovery of our careers," I said. "Susan's issues to the side, it must have some evolutionary reason for targeting human females."

"It will be put down eventually. We don't need to."

"We can't yet," Joiner said.

...

I hunted down an obscure writer living in Colorado who had catalogued thousands of missing persons who had disappeared in the national park system over the years. He put the stories into a series of self-published books that were selling well and making local television news programs. "Eighty-five percent of the missing are women," he told me over the phone. "Generally there is no trace. Just gone, disappeared."

"How long has this been happening?"

"My records go back to the seventies," he said. "Before that, it is difficult to tell."

"Any ideas what has been happening?"

"Theories range from serial killers to UFO's, to be honest with you. The government and law enforcement have had limited success, and because of the nature of the areas—remote, vast, wooded—the resources required to mount a full investigation are just not there. You're talking about hundreds of thousands of square miles. People disappear in the middle of cities and we can't find them, let alone the wilderness. They just have to chalk it up to saying that the woods are dangerous and you should be prepared."

"Any theories of your own?" I asked.

"Interesting," he said. "I thought you were calling to give me yours."

...

The emails were piling up.

Creatures

The National Board of Scientists notified the lab that they were coming. *We have concerns that you may be harboring a newly discovered and possibly dangerous animal at your facility. . . A team of biologists and zoologists will arrive at your facility tomorrow... We expect that you will make every accommodation available to them.*

The thing was groaning and growling in its cage. We tried to feed it raw meat, but it wouldn't eat. Instead it just stood on its hind legs and swayed back and forth like a metronome. Near dinner time, I thought about eating but decided against it. The meat we had thrown into the cage turned my stomach. Instead I decided a walk outside would probably help ease my mind.

Joiner and Shenkstein were in the office. I let myself out through the secured door and saw them sitting at their computers. They weren't working. None of us had really worked since we captured the thing. None of us knew what to say or how to say it. We didn't know what to do. We hadn't even seen it sleep yet. It was just always there. Even when we weren't in the same room we could feel it there. I know I could. And somehow I knew that Joiner and Shenkstein could as well. We all just looked at each other with this strange and profound knowing—a tie that bound us together—the knowledge of *it* and *its* knowledge of us somehow seemed symbiotic.

Joiner laughed, giggling like a school-girl. I asked him what was so funny. He said it was nothing and then started laughing again. Shenkstein had porno on his computer, female flesh being consumed in a different way. "Seriously Dave?" I said. But I let it go. We all sensed an end coming.

"The Feds will be here tomorrow," I said. Joiner laughed. Shenkstein barely grunted over the sound of fake moaning. "Try to look somewhat professional and productive when they get here. This is going to be big news. I'll make sure we get the credit we deserve," I told

99

them. But, really, it was a false hope, and I wasn't sure we deserved any credit at all or should even want it.

"I'll be back later. I need to clear my head."

The Tanzer Facility sat on the edge of a pine forest in the foothills of the Sierra Nevada range. It was still daylight but not for long. I had a good view of the town in the valley below, but I turned my back to it and wandered into the trees. I occasionally hiked out here, the pine needles making each step soft and quiet. I wanted to ease my mind, get clarity. Susan had gone rogue on us. It should have been a coordinated decision by all as to when or how to alert the authorities. Our work hadn't even begun, and now it was going to be taken away.

Maybe not. Maybe I could convince the scientists to let us keep going or to take the lead in the analysis and observation.

I knew I was kidding myself, though. We were a backwater in the biological research world. Frankly, we didn't even have the ability to keep the thing much longer. Maybe we would be allowed to follow through at whatever zoo would house it.

It began to grow dark. Shadows spread from the trees to the entire planet. The sun set on the Pacific, and only the strange dusk of refracted light bounced off the clouds.

And then it stood before me, like it had risen silently right out of the ground. It was on its two legs, so that it was taller than I, and I felt like it had been there with me all along, walking beside me, and I had only just noticed. I felt so strange seeing it there, staring at me with its yellow eyes, swaying back and forth on its heels, its heavy, pendulous forearms swinging dumbly side to side. I wasn't afraid. I was barely surprised. It was like seeing an old friend in a place you never expected; it takes a minute for your mind to catch up, to put the pieces together. You know it's familiar, but you can't place why.

I blinked, and it was gone again. Just like that. It had disappeared—silent, steady, deadly—and I was alone again. But I couldn't get those eyes out of my head, and I noticed that I was swaying on my feet too, left and right. I felt a strange sense of ease, even though, logically, I knew that I had been in mortal danger. I looked around, and it was pitch black night. The air was cold and wet. How could it suddenly be night? How long had I stood here?

And then something horrible dawned on me.

...

The cage was open and Joiner was in the corner laughing like a madman. Shenkstein's eyes hadn't left his computer screen, still flashing flesh and broken moans. The creature was gone.

"What did you do?" I screamed. "What did you do!" I grabbed Joiner and propped him up against the wall. He felt so heavy. His eyes rolled back into his head. Only the whites shone in the night.

"It just walked right by me!" he screamed back. "It just walked right by me!"

The doors were all open. Wind rushed from the mountains, blowing cold air into the lab, lifting reams of data and scattering them like leaves across the floor. I ran to Shenkstein and pushed his head into the computer screen to wake him from his trance. He looked up at me like he had never seen me before in his life.

It was 9:22 p.m. I picked up the landline and racked my brain for Susan's number.

She picked up the phone sounding sleepy.

"Susan," I said. "Susan. . . there's a problem. We have a problem here."

"What?" She was stammering into the phone, her brain rising from its rest. "You're damn right you have a problem there, that's what I've been trying to tell you."

"No. You don't understand." I was trying to find the words but they wouldn't come. It was like I was suddenly left deaf and dumb, my voice just cracking and groaning into the receiver.

"Hold on," she said.

In the background, I could hear the sound of an infant crying in another room. A sound so terribly familiar to me now. Was it Aiden? Was it truly him, or. . .

"Don't, don't, don't. . . " again, I tried.

"Just let me check on the baby," she said. "I'll be right back."

About the Author

Mark Fitch's work has recently appeared in *The Horror Library, Pulp Modern Magazine,* and *Ink Stains*.

*****~~~~~*****

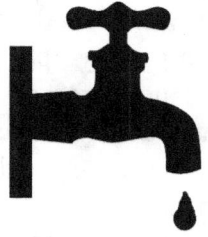

Thirsty Creatures

by Christa Carmen

The trees were fire and the sky was panicked birds and the horse was made of bone.

She knew the horse would not walk forever. She also knew that when the horse could go no further, she would trade her Hell on Earth for one beyond her capacity to conceive.

…

On the day the water turned to poison, she had done the bad thing again. When her mother appeared before her, she was certain it was to scold her for her atrocious, perverted ways. But when her mother opened her mouth, a river of red ran out in place of reproach. In a revelation of horror, she remembered her mother guzzling the glass of water from the faucet, and she gripped her favorite stuffed creature—a gift that she had not deserved—as the gore rushed from between her mother's lips, hiding her face in its fur so she would not have to see.

She heard the muffled thwump when her mother's body hit the floor. By then, her brother had drunk the water too (*by then, who hadn't?*), and when he saw their mother in a frothy sea of unrelenting red, he opened his mouth to scream. His insides came out instead of sound.

Strange Beasties

She watched as the mundane setting of their living room became an estuary of brackish blood, her brother's red mixing with her mother's. The book that had taught her about brackish water and estuaries and other interesting, scientific things lay open on her desk upstairs. It would remain there now, for an eternity. Unless the water cleared and there was anyone left to drink it.

When the bottled water had been reduced to a wasteland of empty plastic, she braced herself to venture outside. Outside, where the world rained ash and the wind blew pain. It was also where the well ran deep, and if she was lucky, ran clean.

She was desperate for a drink, but recalled the book on her desk, extolling the scientific method and the testing of hypotheses. With her tongue like a shed carapace in her mouth, and her innards like sand in a sieve, she crouched behind the stone wall and settled in to *observe*.

When to delay another second would be a fate worse than what waited for her in the kitchen tap, a raven fluttered down to perch on the bait: a bucket of water exhumed from the well's depths. The great black bird lowered its head to sip, and splashed water over its wings. She held her breath, waiting for a rivulet of red to spew from its throat, to wrack its fragile, feathered body. The raven opened its beak, but only a song emerged, and she wept with relief. The salty tears made her thirstier than ever.

She filled every container she could find with unspoiled water from the well. An old tomcat mewled and hissed and spat, and though she lamented his misfortune, she could not share such a precious commodity with a cat. She reminded herself that she was wicked and depraved, and she was able to stomach her cruelty more easily.

She carried bucket after bucket of crisp, cool water to the barn, delivering the stores to a single stall. Encompassed in the narrow space was her mother's former show horse, the strongest horse on the farm, of the most impressive breeding. The horse that would fare the best when it came time to abandon their home.

Without water, the milk cow and the donkeys and the other horses fell. Their already dehydrated corpses withered and shrunk, their eye sockets widening to gaping, fly-infested chasms. She was not privy to the noises their bodies made when they collapsed, but she imagined they sounded like her mother had. And like her brother. All things sounded the same when they fell in death.

The morning the well ran dry, the air was thick and smelled of sulfur. She tacked up her mount and filled the saddlebags with bottles and canteens. She left the farm, not bothering to say goodbye. She did bring along her favorite stuffed creature, holding it before her on the horn of the saddle. A sleight of hand to delude herself into believing she did not ride alone.

The earth was blood red and bone dry. She saw no one in the weeks and months after setting out, would have almost welcomed the inconvenience of defending her water supply from fiend or foe. With no one to contend with, the caches of hydration were infinite; abandoned grocery stores reigned over empty parking lots, and households were rife with countless bottles of uncontaminated liquid, foregone by the fallen for the poison-spouting spigots.

There were no budding blossoms or kaleidoscopic foliage with which to judge the passing of the seasons. The horse had long become accustomed to the endless road, its body changing, shifting, ridding itself of useless things like tissue and muscle and flesh. Now the once-show horse was a chrysalis of dust and bone, its ribcage like a steel trap that held its heart hostage.

Her own skin had fused with the horse's hellish hide. She had ridden the wretched beast to the ends of the Earth and back, and would repeat this journey again and again, with no end in sight. The stuffed creature, too, persisted, its body worn to nothing by the friction of her hands, its face erased by kisses from her parched lips. It was a tether to the past and a clue to her future. The faceless, nameless being was a blueprint for her soul.

At first, she prayed to the deities of water, of wells and springs and fountains and rivers, and to the god and queen of the sea. She pleaded with them to release her as they had all the others. But she knew that to pray was to sin, for she knew her punishment was just. It was her fate to have all the water in the world, and no way to douse the fire.

Time disintegrated, and it came to her that she had not required a drink in as long as she could remember. Somewhere along the purgatorial path, she had ceased to possess those qualities that made her human. Water was no longer an essential element. As it were, every drop had long since dried up. Her thirst, however, grew torturous and vast.

If she could only take back the bad thing, she'd have done so in a heartbeat. She would have drunk the poisoned water in her brother's place a thousand times over, and the river of red would have poured from her mouth in place of all her lies.

But. . .

. . .

The trees were fire and the sky was panicked birds and the horse was made of bone.

And she was one with the horse, an empty web of regret. Like the stuffed creature in her arms, her last link to a long-gone world, she was faceless. Formless.

And so very, very thirsty.

###

About the Author

Christa Carmen lives in Westerly, Rhode Island, with her husband and a beagle who rivals her in stubbornness. Her work has appeared in a myriad of anthologies and ezines, including *DarkFuse Magazine* and *Year's Best Hardcore Horror Volume 2*, and she is currently pursuing a Master's in Creative Writing & Literature from Harvard Extension School.

*****~~~~~*****

Harry on the Farm

by Isobel Horsburgh

Isaac wanted to give Harry some of the smoky bacon crisps that his father had got when they stopped at the petrol station in West Denton, but Mr. Grainger said, no better not, he might get travel sick, and anyone being sick in the car was one of the things that made Mummy cross. Isaac wasn't usually allowed crisps, but Mummy wasn't here.

He was the first to see the sea, as they came up to the coast road, and they drove along the broad front at Whitley Bay, but they couldn't see the sand today, because the wall was too high. Isaac had been to the beach a long time ago, summer last year, but not this year because he had to stay in the house and keep Mummy company. He was good at swimming, but the pool had been getting repaired for ages, whenever he asked Daddy if it was time to go there. Harry made a little sniffing noise in his basket, as though he could smell the crisps. Isaac tried to eat them quietly, so he wouldn't be jealous. The crisps made Isaac a bit thirsty, but he didn't want to ask for a coke, because they hadn't got any more time to stop for anyone to go. If Harry needed to go, he was going to have to do it in his basket.

"When Harry goes on the farm, he can have some crisps, can't he, daddy?"

"As many as he likes, I expect." There was St. Mary's lighthouse sticking up at the end of its causeway, and they were pulling away from the houses now, out into fields, and the sky was wide and very blue. There were wide, white clouds as well, that looked like they'd been whipped up in the blender, like when Rosy used to make cakes. Isaac used to help her with that, but she wasn't there now. Mummy said it was a relief to get HER kitchen back, but she only ever made green shakes, for herself. She said white sugar was poison.

"On the farm, Harry can play with Charlie, can't he?"

"Yes, I expect Charlie will be very pleased to see Harry." Isaac's father looked straight ahead when he spoke, because you had to pay attention when you were driving, even when there weren't a lot of cars about, like now.

"When we get to the farm, can I see Charlie, Daddy, only I didn't see Charlie go away at Christmas, he just went off, all by himself?"

Isaac remembered coming downstairs on Boxing Day and finding Rosy crouched wiping up something off the oatmeal carpet under the Christmas tree, and Mummy saying, "It's just one more bloody thing after another. I don't know why I bother. I let myself get talked into this, yet again, and look what happens. It's diabolical. I don't want a stain left, you understand?"

Charlie's red blanket lay nearby, and his squeaky kitty. There was a note for Isaac, on the back of his Christmas list, that Santa must have dropped on his way out of the woodburner (it would have been a tight squeeze, so that explained it), saying, "Sorry, had to dash, another family needs me, love Charlie," and some xxxs. It was written in the same colour as the ink on the label on Isaac's stocking that said "Merry Christmas, love Santa," so Santa must have lent Charlie his pen.

Isaac's father said, "I don't know, 'Zac. Charlie might have gone out for a walk or something, but you can see him, if he's around, I expect."

"But does he not know that we're coming? Doesn't he want to see me?"

"For heaven's sake, Isaac, don't start. You're a very lucky boy, getting to go for a drive like this, in the Audi, instead of having to go on the bus, like some people."

Daddy and Isaac usually laughed together at the thought of them catching the bus. Isaac had been on a train once, in France, but that was all right, because it was a special train for people like them, and nobody else was allowed on. The driver would have thumped anyone who tried to climb aboard. Mummy called people who they saw standing at bus stops, "the great unwashed," so Isaac supposed they must be really special. He'd once asked Rosy if she was one of the great unwashed, because she was special and made singin' hinnies for him, and Mummy had said, "Isaac! That's rude!' but she'd laughed, her hand cupping her glass, light shining though the honey-coloured bubbles. Her fingernails were pearly pink, and if she broke one, it was, she said, a real tragedy. She said if Rosy would lay off the singin' hinnies, she might lose a bit of weight. Isaac didn't think Rosy was fat. She was good at cuddles. He told Mummy that, and her face went all sucked-lemon. It wasn't long after, that Rosy went.

They were really out in the country now, and the farm couldn't be very far. Harry was not asleep, but very quiet. Isaac could see his shiny eyes, through the holes in the side of the basket. He must be thinking to himself about his new home. This was the best thing for him, really, Daddy said, because there wasn't as much room to run around in their garden now, with the hot tub coming. Isaac had said, "couldn't he run around in the house?"

"Not really, because the men are coming to make the spa, and Harry would get underfoot."

111

"But if I kept him in my room, he wouldn't be underfoot."

"Don't be silly, Isaac, you're not a baby." He was almost seven, which was the magic number. He used to hear Mummy and Daddy talk about it.

"Daddy. . . "

"Now what?"

"Will Mimi be there, on the farm, with Charlie? And Olly? And Bobby and Ben? Or will they all have gone for a walk, together?"

"Christ, Isaac, will you give it a rest?" Daddy's hair was a bit like a halo from the back, fair and fluffy around the pink bit, now that the light was catching it. Rosy had lovely dark hair that she hoiked up with a silvery clip when she was cooking. She said she was a bit of a Gypsy. She called Isaac her bairn, before she left. Mummy said, "Gypsy Rose Dobson didn't see that coming."

They were coming up to Kielder, now, to the forest. The forest was different from other forests, because it was dark all year 'round. The leaves never changed to orange. They were carnivorous. They didn't have bears and wolves here, which was a pity, because it would have been a great place for them to hide, and lots of people came to do sailing on the reservoir, and bird watching, so they could always have got something to eat. They wouldn't have eaten Isaac's family, they would have gone after people having takeaways, who were fat and slow, and who Mummy said smelt of chips.

"Here we are, Isaac, out you get." Mr. Grainger leaned over and helped Isaac with the buckle of his seat belt. Harry gave a whimpering sound as though he was a bit puzzled. Isaac scrambled out, and stood and looked around the car park. The picnic tables were empty. All the fat people must have gone home to have chips for dinner. The heavy dark trees were all around, stiff as pencils, all in a row. Daddy was still in the front seat, and Harry's

112

basket was in the back. Daddy was rummaging in the glove compartment.

"Hurry up, Daddy."

"Well, you'll have to run."

"What?"

"Run up to the farm, and tell them we're on our way. It's just over there."

Isaac peered about him. "It's dark, nearly!"

"All the more reason to hurry. Straight ahead of you, down the path, you can't miss it."

"Why aren't you coming with me?"

"Because I have to make an important call, as soon as I find my phone. I'm sure it's here somewhere."

"Can't you make an important call, and come with me?"

"Not carrying Harry, I can't."

"Can't he just walk?'

'No, he's too little. And I can't leave him by himself."

"I can carry him. He's not very heavy yet."

"What did I say about not being a baby? Mummy wouldn't be happy about this. We mustn't upset her."

Isaac kept looking back over his shoulder at the Audi as he stumbled along the path. There was nothing much growing under the trees, just bare brown earth, like the floor of a cave. Tunnels among the trees opened up on either side of the path. It was getting harder to see his way. There were no wolves, there were no bears. They only like the smell of chips, and sweeties. He wasn't allowed sweets. Rosy used to give him cinder toffee. It stuck in his teeth. She made gingerbread men in red and white strips, like the Black Cats wore. He thought it would be good if they really were cats and played footie, but really they were only men. If there really was a gingerbread house in the forest, the bears would eat it. What if the witch was in the loo, and bears came and ate the house? She would be cross, if people saw her in there.

He wouldn't laugh, in case she said he was rude. There wasn't a witch. If she was as thin as a stick, from not eating, she could stand behind a tree. That tree, or that one.

He walked up the middle of the path, trying not to look at the trees. He thought if the farm had lots of animals, he might hear them. He stood and listened, squeezing his eyes half-shut to keep the trees out, for cows mooing. There was nothing making noises, nothing alive. He set off back the way he had come. The light was draining away. He hoped Daddy wouldn't play war with him, felt his breath tight in his chest from hurrying. Here it was again, at last, the car park. He stood and stared across the tarmac. There were no cars left in the car park. There was no Audi.

On the other side of the reservoir, in a lay-by, Ewan Grainger was sitting with his phone, and a thermos flask. Harry nestled drowsily against him, squirming a little.

"You'd hardly know him, Rose, he's changed so much since you left. I almost left it too late with this one, thinking it can't be going to happen again, or there's another way, a way out, but there never is. We were all set to celebrate the big birthday, the magic one, the one that meant it wasn't going to happen, that we'd got safely through. And then I saw him standing by the fishpond in the park, chewing something, the light shining through his ears. There was green stuff, strands of weed on his teeth. I keep asking myself, did it happen overnight, or was I just not looking properly? We'd been keeping him away from the deep water, it sounds silly, but we felt, you know, it might somehow call it out of him. Even now, after all the others, I don't really know how it works. I only know, if people found out, they'd blame us somehow, take the little one away. I can't do that to Sinead.

"It never gets any easier, even though I know this is the right thing to do. I've not slept for days, hardly. I can

114

barely keep my eyes open, I'm not really safe to drive. Sinead's so brittle, she looks as if she could just snap in half. I wish you'd known her the way she used to be, before all this. She scarcely ever leaves the house now. She blames herself, and of course it's not her fault, it's the genes." On the far side of the moonlit reservoir, there was a ripple of movement.

"He's just drained the strength out of her, and he doesn't know he's doing it. He would have done the same to you, you know. I wish I could take some of it on myself, but it doesn't seem to work like that. It never has. No, I've told you, you shouldn't have got so close." Out on the water, a sleek V was gliding across the pewter surface. Harry's wide eyes followed it.

Nearby, catching the edge of the yellow circle thrown by the headlights, a wreath of bubbles frothed, and then was still. Harry stirred, gazing, and gave a small enquiring squeak.

"Shh, good lad. No, Rose, our only hope is that it's the magic number, lucky seven. We've got to hang on to what we've got left. We've lost so much, we deserve to be lucky just once. Sinead deserves that. Yes, later, I'll call you tomorrow, bye."

Black coffee from the flask wasn't enough to keep him awake. Ewan felt his eyes closing, reached for the radio switch. Harry's brown eyes were fixed on the long muzzle breaking the surface. Ewan's head drooped. Harry felt him slump, listening to the murmuring of the radio. Raindrops spattered the windshield. In the darkness a bird shrieked, just once.

After a time, a small, upright figure came and stood by the Audi, shaking spray from its mane, flicking droplets from its pointed ears. It wore a T-shirt with Count Duckula on the front, and knee-length shorts. The feet were bare and rounded, without toes, something between a flipper and a hoof. Silver-green eyes with long, frosted lashes looked in at the window, a hand gripped the door-handle. The door was yanked open. Fingers, lightly webbed, closed around Harry's fleecy mitten. Wide nostrils flared, breath sweet-smelling and redolent of potato crisps. The long head turned and nodded towards the black expanse of water.

"Don't worry, Harry, I think Daddy's gone to sleep, but we're going to go together and find the farm."

About the Author

Isobel Horsburgh lives on South Tyneside, in North East England. She used to be a long-term carer, and she now does casual work in libraries. She volunteers for the British Heart Foundation, the Willows Cat Rescue, and the North East Mining Institute. Her work has appeared in *Space Squid, Devilfish Review, BlinkInk, The Drabble, The Casket Of Fictional Delights, Urban Fantasist, 200cc, It's All Trumped Up, Phobos, Gathering Storm*, and *Noir: At The Salad Bar.*

*****~~~~~*****

Sailors' Hearts Taste Better

by Paulo da Silva

The only perk to being eternally cursed as a saltwater siren is that the hearts I devour at least have some seasoning.

Poor Nalia, that young nymph, still languishing in sweet waters, is losing color from an anemic diet of insipid livers and savorless kidneys.

"But I want to capture a man who shall take my curse away, Leodora," she says to me. "Such a strapping young fellow surely cannot be found on the high seas."

Ah, the lass—so young, so naive, so romantically quaint—holds on hopelessly to the remnants of her once-human life.

"The men of the brine," I rasp, "those who suffer the Black, the tempests, the turmoil and maelstroms; those with leathered skins and calloused hands—these are *men,* my young Nalia. Their hearts are cold and their fibers tough. And once the ocean pickles them, one is enough to keep you nourished for months."

"I do not want nourishment. I want *love.*" Her freshwater eyes twinkle under dappled sunlight. Her blond hair glows with enchanted serenity and promise. Her skin, so pale, so innocent, so untouched, glistens like mother-of-pearl.

Not like me. I have moray eels for hair. My once-supple skin is now toughly armored in scales to overcome the jaws of leviathans or the tentacles of krakens. My breasts are stonefish; my eyes, sea wasps. I am the most dangerous predator of the sea.

But not to *them*—to my lovers, my sea dogs, my bluejackets and shellbacks. To them I am the Answer, I am She, Her, the One. I am Glory and Promise. I am the waters, enticing and loving, *and I will bring you home, my sailor. Come to me. Come. Come. Jump into my depths and sink down into the murky netherland of drowned sorrows, to your fulfilled marine destiny. Come to me, my mate, my middy, my mariner.*

They fill my stomach, and yet never reach the caverns of my heart.

"I am glad that you visit me," says Nalia on the bank, brushing perfect hair to cover breasts yet untouched by gravity. "I have no other friends. I am so. . . alone."

"I am only here to show you the truth of what you are. I want to introduce you to Alexandra and Ekho and Gaia, others like us, all once fresh like you, but now all pickled. You need not be alone, Nalia."

"Do they look like you as well?" Her lip twists up into a grimace.

I am not insulted.

And then—

Oh, yes, I smell one, sawdust and sweat, a suitor in the woods, maybe a mile away, two at most.

It's the hair brushing that does it, sending pheromones of bedazzlement to any who cares to reach for them. I had a brush once. But now, my mere existence brings them to me.

In a moment, the bait will be standing behind that oak tree, rubbing his eyes, wondering if what he sees is sooth. And Nalia will converse with him, believing his desire to be one of True Love.

Nalia stops brushing. She can feel him, too. Her breathing deepens, her lips part, her cheeks rouge. "Oh, Leodora, could he be the one? Could he? Could he!" Sweat gleams on her brow.

I push against the riverbank, float backwards into the rushing water. "Nalia, follow this water west with me, and we'll collide with the estuary and break the barrier between sweet and salt. Only food matters for our kind, dear."

"No, no, I cannot. Not now. Not when he approaches! He shall cure me, Leodora. He shall bring me back to life again with his True Love, not like the others. I can feel it."

"You will eat his heart when you find his desires to be soiled, just like the others."

"No, no, I won't, not this one, he shall shatter the curse, he shall—"

A twig snaps behind her. She gasps. But only a deer appears.

His scent is stronger now, closer. Musk, the mouth-watering stink of a day's toil. Not a dandy, this one; hard, a worker. By the gods, could the freshwater meat be as gritty as that of my deck hands?

No; not a chance, not—

Nalia senses my thoughts, feels my growing hunger for him. She jolts onto her feet. "He's mine!" she screams, fists clenched, body trembling, blue eyes riveted to the snapping eels on my head.

"Get away, you hag!" She hurls the brush at me, but it misses. "You monster! You are vile, horrible, ugly and grotesque! I will never become like you!"

Ah, dear lass, you already are. Inside, we are both the same.

"It does not matter how we look on the outside, Nalia. They see what they want to see. They see their own lust when they look at us."

"You lie! You lie! You—" She grabs a rock, flings it.

The stone cracks my forehead, and red ichor filters my vision, its downpour spicing up the sweetwater. I lick it, priming my tongue for the imminent flavor of copper.

"I will prove I am not like you," she says. "You *eel,* you. . . *oyster slime.*"

Ah. The bloody lass. So damned naive.

The man arrives.

Nalia bares herself to him—a glorious sight, she is, if only she understood how much.

But his eyes do not see her. He looks beyond her shoulder. *Come to me, riverman. Come. Come. Come.*

Nalia's abject scream pierces the sky in counterpoint to the man's splash into the water. *Yes. Good man.* Then she howls, crashes to her knees, weeps. The sounds are a symphony, and his moans furnish the percussion. My eels hiss—the wind instruments. My scales clatter like cymbals, and then, finally, the crescendo, ending with the shattering snap of my jaws as I crush his neck, rip down through his flesh, and tear out his insipid heart with shark teeth.

The tang of Nalia's sorrow engulfs me, puckering my ventral skin and agitating my gills.

Nalia's brackish tears cascade into the river, until it deluges over the bank, ebbing and flowing toward her outstretched feet, licking at her guileless toes like the merciful tentacles of an undiscriminating squid, ready to bring her into the juices of our subsuming sea; ready to make her one with the water, a single zooid in the colonial organism which comprises our accursed souls—none of us able to survive alone, but together deadlier than any perfidious Lothario who seeks merely to skim superficial pleasure from the surface-waters of our youthful skins before harpooning anguish into the depths of our misled hearts.

120

I, too, sat in her position once, chest wracked by sobs.

The moon rises, and the river runs cold. My teeth clatter, but their bone-sound is nothing to the wail of horror ejected by the girl on the shore who suffers a broken heart.

I am here, child.

The sun awakens.

I float, ventral skin up, arms sinking down into the cool where a million droplets converge into one torrential current, surging in the direction of an ocean whose waters might be made only of tears.

The sobbing eases down to resigned whimpers. And then to silence.

Ah, lass, I believe in you.

Splash!

I knew she could do it.

Nalia swims underneath me, grazes delicate fingers over my caudal fin, up to the iridescence of my back, runs a trembling hand through the now-quieted morays on my head. The eels curl around her wrist and slither over unblemished skin, caressing it, welcoming her into the abyssal dark.

The ends of her hairs split into mouths containing rear-hooked teeth, expand into globules of tiny heads. Her breasts swell and sag, then darken to the color of hardy stones. Her hips widen, her legs transmute into a scintillating wave of scale-adorned billowing magnificence.

She is gorgeous.

And then she sees it.

Her eyes, glistening pearls, stare aghast at my form, suddenly not believing. Her breath quickens with unexpected excitement.

She has learned it, as I learned it from Alexandra who learned it from Ekho who learned it from Gaia. There is unseen beauty in the depths, obscured on the surface water by duplicitous reflections.

"Leodora, by the gods, I cannot—I cannot believe my eyes! You are—you are—you are *ravishing*!"

I bring my hand to her dorsal fin, stroke it. "Nay, lass. I am as I was; only your view has changed."

"I wish to look like you, Leodora. I wish to command the bottomless beauty that you do!"

"You already do, my Nalia. In my eyes you have always been exquisite."

We surge west, undulating shadows disappearing into the dark, fingers interlocked, seeking sustenance to fill our stomachs, confident that the caverns of our hearts might never feel empty again.

About the Author

Paulo da Silva has written fiction under four different pseudonyms, two genders, and six genres. This has nothing to do with the fact that he is Portuguese, was raised in South Africa, lives in Germany, and works mostly for a UK company. One day he hopes to live in the Bahamas. He has recently published works in *Soulmonger* and *Daily Science Fiction.*

*****~~~~~*****

The Passenger

by Jeff Hewitt

Henry Grimwall drove through the sleet with the caution of an old hand. The headlights did little to pierce the dark. His wipers struggled to keep up with the downpour. Henry took his time. He found his thoughts slipping towards the bag in his trunk, unable to ignore its presence like a piece of dust in his eye. The radio whispered, almost inaudible under the sound of the wipers and the driving sleet. The back roads dipped and turned. Tall, dark trees lined the curving, two-lane road as it snaked through the countryside. He kept his eyes sharp for deer and other roadside menaces, but even they were hunkered down somewhere out of this mess. Henry came to a four-way stop and turned left. As his lights swept the ground across from the stop sign, he saw something—someone—in the ditch.

He pulled over and turned on his emergency lights. Someone in the ditch out in this! He pulled out his cell phone to call for help, but the screen read "No Service." *That's right*, he thought. Henry pulled his heavy overcoat tight and got out. The sleet soaked him, stealing his breath and forcing a shiver. He got out a little pocket flashlight and shined it down. There it is. A person wrapped up in a thick coat much like his own, lying in the ditch. *It must be a man*, he thought. At least six something and 300 pounds. He knelt, reached out a hand, and touched the man on the shoulder.

"Hey pal, you okay?" He shook the man with soft movements. The coat was thick with ice. Just as Henry was convinced that he'd discovered a body (and now what to do with it!) the man groaned.

"Hey! You're alive! Come on, get in my car. You're going to freeze out here!" He helped the man to his feet and walked him to the car. The man leaned on him. *This must be what the natives felt moving those Easter Island heads around,* he thought. Henry opened the passenger door of his car and helped the man in. His breath frosted the air as he got back into his car. The stranger had wrapped his arms around himself and was shivering. Henry reached down and turned the heat all the way up, grateful for the warmth. *I just put a stranger in my front seat,* he thought.

The two men shivered and huffed in the car as the heat thawed them out. Henry shed his coat after a moment and stuffed it in the backseat. He was soaked around his collar and waist, but at least he wasn't drenched like the stranger next to him.

"I think I've got a warm sweater or something that might fit you, at least until your clothes dry. I'm Henry, by the way." Henry's breath caught in his throat when the stranger finally turned to look at him. His eyes. . . *its* eyes. . . were solid black and ringed with gold. Its face was scaled and plated.

"My. . . my God. . . "

"Not your god. Thank you for the warmth." The creature's voice rumbled deep in its chest.

"Don't hurt me, please. I've got a family." The creature rumbled again, but despite Henry's terror, he thought he detected humor in it.

"I won't hurt you. You gave me a place to warm up. It's not our way."

"Your way?"

"What once was our way, I suppose."

"What are you?"

124

"I am. . . you would say monster, or perhaps elemental, but from a place and time. . . long ago." The creature turned its head.

"What are you doing out here?"

"It's a crossroads. I came here to die. The last place where I thought I might feel at home before the end."

"You're dying?" The creature nodded its ponderous head. How could Henry have mistaken it for a man at all?

"Are you sick?"

"In a manner of speaking. The world turned old. Forgot the young things, the monsters and stories and people from long ago."

"You're a young thing? How long have you been alive?"

"That's. . . difficult to answer. We reckon time different from you. I remember. . . " The creature's eyes turned glassy. Its voice rumbled. "Drive on to your destination. I'll leave soon enough." It looked off into the darkness of the forest as the trees rushed by. It finally broke the long silence.

". . . I remember a time when there were no people here. The land was young, and hot. The trees grew and grew. Great conspiracies and nations of trees, whispering in the vastness. I could walk for days and never see another one of my people. Kingdoms rose and fell. Kingdoms of animals, kingdoms of fairyfolk. . . then humans came. Small, squat, grunting with their foreign voices. At first, just a few, then more, then more, and then many. I remember a time when you could walk the Mississippi and hear a new language every day. You could wake up in one nation and bed down in another. And they loved us, those early humans. With the world turning and changing, they looked to us for knowledge. Prayed to us. Prayer is a funny thing. Has anyone ever prayed to you?"

"Not that I know of."

"It changes you. When people ask for your help, for your blessings and knowledge, the weight of their needs presses on you. Changes you. Like coal into diamonds. For a long time we wandered the world, gods amongst the humans. And then there was a time when they all disappeared. They got sick. I'd walk the rivers and streams and see no one at all. I found villages of ghosts. Places where once many people walked and sang and lived were now haunts for the birds and the conspiracies of trees. Spiders wove webs in cradles. Vines brought the houses back to the Earth. And this was the first time I got sick as well."

"You never got sick?"

"Not before the humans prayed to me. Before, I was part of the landscape. How does a rock get sick? The wind does not sneeze. But then I was given shape and form. Prayed to. Changed. I had hands and scales and feet. And sickness came. The people who were left, the lost ones, started to fill up the land again; but not as fast as before. Then the horses came. The world was wild. The horses made everything different and new again." Henry came to a lonely light, flashing yellow in the dark.

"Do you want me to drop you off somewhere?"

"I. . . I want to tell it all. If I may. Someone has to hear it all told, or it will die with me."

"It's about another thirty minutes from here, where I'm headed. I don't mind the company," Henry replied.

"Thank you."

"So, the horses came?"

"Yes. They made the world fast and full of life. It was more thoughtful before them, a slow place. Tangled, and verdant, but not alive in the way the horses were. They ran and ran and ran, huge herds of them, as many as you could see from the top of a tall hill. They brought thunder to the clear skies. That was a time to be alive. I was not as great as before. The horses changed that, but I

126

was still important, too. I began to revive. I was wan for so long that I felt like I was being born again."

"And then the time came. The last of the people to come across the sea, and my world changed again. The sickness returned, and guns came. You can't imagine how hearing a gun for the first time changed the world. Seeing the carnage wrought, struck down by the invisible force of a gun. They pressed towards the other great ocean, and the land was brought to heel. The people changed. They became less. No one prayed to us anymore. We were replaced with gods of steel and coal and steam and fire. And the Christ, of course. The world became mechanical, and there was only one man to pray to. We died slowly, like a flower in the fall."

"Are there any of your people left?"

"I don't know. It's been so long since I've seen anyone. I think I am the last, or one of them. It's the time for me to be done."

"Is there no way for you to go on?"

"I don't think so. I feel so thin now. I feel myself returning to the Earth, like a long sleep. There are days I think I can see through myself. I lay down and when I get up the season is different. It's time to rest."

They came to a gate at the end of a gravel road.

"This is the end of my road, friend."

"Is there a place I could lay down?"

"There is a hot spring deep in the property, if you think that would work." The creature's eyes seemed to light up.

"That would be perfect."

Henry got out of the car and unlocked the gate, then swung it open. They bumped down the gravel road. The sleet gave one last fitful spray as they pulled up to a handsome log cabin and stopped. The world had an ethereal glow in the way that only cold water in headlights can have. The man and the monster got out of the vehicle.

"If you don't mind, I'll join you at the hot spring. That was my intention for this visit," said Henry.

"It would be good to have someone with me, at the end." The creature seemed to shiver. "Even one such as me dreads coming to the end alone."

Henry hurried into the cabin and came out a moment later in a thick robe. He reached back inside the door and flipped a switch. A string of lights came on, illuminating a gravel path in a cool glow. Henry walked to his car and popped the trunk. He took out a small overnight bag. He motioned for the creature to follow him. They crunched through the woods, Henry's breath fogging in thick clouds of white. The clouds blew off the moon, and it added its own faint white light to the journey. The trees were stark and leafless in that gentle light. The trees had once reminded Henry of claws and broken bones grasping at the sky, but tonight they were somehow less menacing.

After a few minutes of walking, they arrived at the hot spring. It was a large round pool, with fog and steam coming off it in torrents. The air had a faint sulfurous smell. The creature's reptilian face broke into a wide smile.

"What a perfect place to come to the end! You have something beautiful here."

"Thank you. I always come here when the weight of everything is too much for me." Henry set the travel bag down at the end of a little deck that had been built around the spring and took off his robe. His skin shone in the moonlight. The creature stripped off its heavy coat and appeared naked as well, but in the nature of lizards it was difficult to determine a sex.

"Please go in first," said Henry. The creature slipped into the hot water with the practiced ease of a predator in its element. It disappeared up to its neck, and its head alone in the water thrilled Henry, as it looked so much like a huge alligator. He slipped into the hot water himself. The heat enveloped him. He groaned with pleasure.

"Does my bones good." The creature nodded and swirled about in the water a few times, stirring up a fresh smell of hot rocks and minerals.

"This is delicious after being so cold," it said.

"I imagine. Are you cold-blooded?"

"I'm not sure what that means."

"It means. . . ah. . . you derive heat from outside of yourself. Like by laying in the sun, or on hot rocks."

"Oh. Well, I suppose I am. Or was."

"Was?"

"They once made sacrifices to me."

"The people who worshiped you?"

"Yes."

"What did they sacrifice?"

"All kinds of things. At first it was small things. A bowl of fruit. A fat chicken. And then they decided that I wanted them hot, fresh, with blood flowing. They sacrificed people to me. The first few I remember well. Young women, it always seemed to be. Girls. They figured out it's better to sacrifice someone else eventually. Started killing other humans, taking them from others and bringing them to me."

"You remember the first one?"

"Oh, yes. I think that's when I woke up for the first time. Really woke up. I remember the taste of her blood. She was a young thing. Dark and small and wild, so wild."

"Did you eat her?"

"No. . . no. . . that's an interesting question. I never have. Never eaten anyone. I could just taste the blood, felt it heating me up from the inside. I don't even think I was there for it. It just happened. At one moment, I existed in a sense within the earth, aware but only barely, and sleeping. The next, blood is pouring down my gullet and I'm awake and alive and here."

"So, there's power in the blood?"

"More than anywhere else, concentrated power, there."

"I understand a lot of gods wanted that."

"Yes. I remember once going south. South, south, south. I was turned back, one day. I walked down the Mississippi and came to the end of it, but I wanted to keep going south. I could feel the draw of the power, you understand. Something like a song written in writhing blood. So much power! I went south, drawn to it. I walked the deserts of Mexico, tasted new sacrifices, met strange gods. We were all drawn south. I came to the jungles, then. They were so thick. You couldn't move at times the undergrowth was so thick. The cats prowled in the shadows, watching me. Many things to me today are fuzzy, or hard to remember, but not this. The song was so loud, it near made me insane. I think at that time I saw others of my kind, little gods and creatures drawn to the power.

"And I saw it, finally, saw it: the place where the power flowed. It was a pyramid, squares on top of squares, and at the top, a radiant sun of blood red. And above that, a great god. Huge, and hungry. The people here gave him beating hearts, fed him constantly. The god was fat and gorged and soaked in the blood of his people, and still more he gobbled. We, the little gods, converged on that place. Some, I think, even got a taste of that font. Then the big god noticed us. It was terrible. I cannot speak of it, the feeling of a god such as that looking at you. The world stops, and the universe has a center, and it is *you*. It was for only a moment, and yet, it was also forever.

"The terrible gaze held me in that brief moment, and I learned true fear, then. I fled all the way back here. To the place where the little gods were safe. I remember hearing a terrible darkness behind me, even though that didn't make sense. I think that god drank the blood of some of my people that day. I've never been that far south again."

130

The night was still. The hot springs hissed and bubbled. The two soaked. Then the creature spoke.

"Why did you come out here, in the middle of the night, Henry?"

Henry sighed. "Can you hear my thoughts?"

"No. I am no such being."

"I came here to die, same as you."

"Really? Are you ill as well?"

"Maybe. I think I understand some of your feelings. Feeling wan. Feeling thin, and lost. I have felt that way most of my life. So many others knew what they wanted to do their whole lives, and I never have. I'm into my forties, and if you asked me what I wanted to do with my life I'd still say 'I don't know.' I feel no passion. There are things I care about, sure. I love my wife. . . my children. Yet, it is a disinterested care. I feel at times I could drift away, or they could, lost in an ocean of emotionless water. Would I mind? I don't know. I feel like a passenger in my own life. How do I confront the decision to die? With disinterest. I wonder if I will feel pain, if I will fade away. I wonder if I will live on, in a hell or a heaven or in a void somewhere. Will I be reborn? I don't know. What is one bland hell, one uninteresting heaven? Do I live in one now? This could be purgatory. I experience a thin veneer of life, mixed good and bad, until it is time for me to move on. Perhaps there is a grieving family in the real world and they are praying for me. I came here to die, and see if there was any difference."

"Do you think there will be?"

"No. I think this is it. Perhaps I will enter a black void. If that was all there was, would I know the difference?"

"What of your family?"

"They will be comfortable. There's a good bit of money tucked away, and I have made as many arrangements as I could. They will be taken care of.

Ultimately that's all I was doing before." Henry shifted in the hot water. Sweat poured down his face.

"I will miss my wife, I think, if I am in any position to do so. She is something else. Perhaps the only thing that I can think of that makes me hesitate."

"Is she a good wife?"

"The best. She always takes care of me. Makes sure I am presentable, holds me when I need it. She knows a special way to take the pain away. I am not disinterested in her, but madly in love."

"Then why choose to die?"

"I feel much like I am trapped beneath the surface of a frozen lake. I am numb, and ready to drift away. She is a straw, breaking the ice, letting me breathe, but for how long can I stay alive drawing such small breaths?"

They sat in the hot water for a long time. Somewhere in the woods, an owl broke the silence with a single forlorn hoot.

"I think it's time," said Henry. He waded to the overnight bag and drew out a bottle and a razor.

"How will you do it?"

"I am going to drink this first. It's a very fine whiskey. Then I will cut open my veins and let my life flow out. It should be nearly painless, like going to sleep in a hot bath. And then my cares will be gone. And I will see what there is."

Henry took a deep drink. The world grew warmer, fuzzier somehow. The god was close to him, now. Its eyes were on him with such interest and intensity he felt for a moment how this creature must have when the terrible bloody god looked at it. Henry faded in and out of awareness. With his last bit of strength and focus, he gripped the razor, and cut. He didn't feel a thing. His heart thudded in his ears, sluggish and weak. He closed his eyes, but they popped open of their own accord.

The god's face filled his vision.

"How does it feel?"

132

"Like. . . drifting. . . " He felt a heavy pressure on his chest, saw the creature's clawed hand splayed over his heart.

"Listen, Henry. Your family needs you. Your wife loves you. I can feel this in your blood. Give up no hope, but thrive on my blood." The creature slashed open its own veins. Thick, hot blood flowed out in spurts. Henry felt something cover his mouth and flow into his throat, and he choked. The burning hot liquid, so much hotter than the whiskey, pulsed into him, filled him.

"Please don't die," a voice rumbled in the darkness. "Please don't die. It is not yet time."

He awoke the next morning, still up to his neck in the hot spring. Henry felt different. Renewed. Revived. Full of life and interest. The world held special focus and intensity. He looked about himself. He was alone! Where had the creature gone, after everything? A thought struck him. He closed his eyes, and prayed.

Wherever you are, whatever you were, thank you. He sat in the hot spring for a long time, his eyes closed, his soul open and still. He felt the wisps of steam coming off the surface of the spring. He felt the tiny currents lick at his wrists. He heard the rustle of creatures in the woods, heard the cardinals landing on branches, walking in snow. The world held so much! He must learn more. And then he felt it, just a tiny voice, or a whisper. A feeling of welcome. A feeling of gratitude. When he opened his eyes again, he saw a rock that had not been there the night before. It was across the spring from the deck. It looked, if you let the light hit it just right, a lot like the head of an alligator. He waded over to the rock and placed a hand on it. He felt warmth, and friendship. This was now and would forever be a good place. A place of healing.

Henry climbed out of the spring and pulled on his robe. He walked back to the cabin, marveling at the beauty that surrounded him. When he got to the cabin, he heard the phone inside ringing. He hurried in and answered it.

"Hello? Yes, yes I'm fine. I'm sorry about that note, it's weird isn't it? I had a long day at the office and it seemed to make sense at the time. I'm sorry to have worried you. You don't know how sorry. I'm at the cabin, I drove all night. No, I'm not doing anything crazy. I just needed a soak. I'm on my way home. I love you, too." He hung up the line and stared into the rising sun, his eyes strong and bright.

"What a beautiful day."

About the Author

Jeff Hewitt's work has been featured in *Pseudopod,* Cohesion Press, and Third Flatiron Publishing. He's a school teacher by day and a horror author by night.

*****~~~~~*****

Beast of the Month

by Wulf Moon

Dear Beast of the Month Club:

I have truly enjoyed purchasing your beasts over the past few months. Your prices are significantly cheaper compared to some of the local menageries, and your selection is far superior. Your Gurgling Gargoyle has made a handsome addition to my moat, and my recent purchase of the Palm-Sized Salamander made me the envy of the realm. While other wizards have to snatch coals from the hearth to light their pipes, I just give my salamander a squeeze and the tobacco in the bowl glows like a forge. I really have to thank you for this marvelous little beastie. (Do you offer an asbestos carrying case for it? I once made the unfortunate mistake of carrying the critter loose in my pocket.)

That said, I do have one complaint. I recently received a parcel containing a beast I did not order. I am quite certain I sent you last month's reply card, checking the NO box on the featured selection, whatever it might have been.

Please credit me on your invoice and provide instructions for return.

Sincerely,
Wizard Garmon Tokkash
Master, Third Helix

135

...
Dear Subscryer:

We regret that you do not wish to retain the beast we sent you. Our featured selections are always chosen from our most popular inventory, and we are certain you will be pleased if you just give the beast a chance. It's known as a Horrum Kathaar, a massive lycanthrope with a penchant for poetic verse, extremely rare. In order to acquire these magnificent specimens, our buyers risked their lives by passing through the Myrak Portal, barely escaping the Seven Sniveling Sisters, whose endless begging and whining can cause even the staunchest wizards to burst into tears, quite literally. It is a wonder we were able to obtain these beasts to offer our subscryers at all.

However, if you still decide you do not wish to keep the beast, you may return the unopened box to the address listed below, and we will cheerfully credit your account.

Sincerely,
Beast of the Month Club

...
Dear Beast of the Month Club:

We have a problem. I trust we will be able to resolve it amicably. While waiting for your reply, my wife heard pitiful cries issuing from the box, and she thought it only humane to break the seal and make sure the beast was fed and watered. Unfortunately, it appears the pathetic puppy dog whimpering was a ploy. The hairy Horrum Ka-thing escaped, thumping about the corridors on all fours, bellowing the most rude limericks at my wife. It took exquisite delight in spraying every bedpost and newel with its ghastly smelling scent glands, shredded every tapestry in our castle, soiled priceless Perogian rugs, and chewed up my imported Nikay slippers. We have been unable to corner the beast, and it seems impervious to our spells.

Please teleport one of your wizards to help us repackage the beast and repair the damages, and we will be more than happy to return it.

Sincerely,
Wizard Garmon Tokkash
Master, Third Helix

...

Dear Subscryer:

If you didn't want the beast, why did you open the box? We cannot accept returns of used merchandise.

Regretfully,
Beast of the Month Club

...

Dear BMC:

This is outrageous! I just received another beast yesterday, and I DID NOT ORDER IT! What's more, this beast figured out how to break the seal on its own. Together with the Horrible Kathaar, they've hunted down all my other beasts and—with the aid of the salamander they stole from me—have turned them all into barbecue!

Effective immediately, I am canceling my membership to the Beast of the Month Club. If you do not teleport someone instantly to help me contain these malevolent monsters, I will be forced to take action against you. You can be sure the Beastmaster Business Bureau will hear about this matter!

Up yours,
Wizard Garmon Tokkash
Master, Third Helix

...

Dear Subscryer:

Our Collections Department has asked us to remind you that your account is past due. Failure to pay in a timely manner can have serious consequences. Please deposit your payment today in the conveniently provided coffer. If you have already sent your payment, thank you.

As to your correspondence about reporting us to the Beastmaster Business Bureau, that is certainly your right as a conjurer. However, you will find we acquired the BBB as one of our subsidiary companies in a takeover last week. In short, we are your first, last, and only hope of solving your problem with unwanted beasts. May we suggest that you change the tone of your correspondence?

We will continue to send you beasts and charge your account until you have fulfilled your obligation to purchase thirteen beasts. You must meet the terms of the agreement. Failure to do so can result in serious consequences.

Sincerely,
Beast of the Month Club

...

Dear BMC:

Look, you toad-faced wizard wannabes! Another beast just materialized in my courtyard, and he wasn't even contained! After busting off my stone gargoyles and lobbing them at my fleeing servants, these beasts of yours ravaged all the livestock on my estate! As if that wasn't enough, my neighbors scryed me today saying that your unrestrained beasts are eating all of *their* beasts, and they demand that I do something about it! While I am happy the neighbor's harpy is no longer defecating in my moat, I order you to take your beasts back at once and make adequate reparation for damages.

I don't care how powerful you think you are. Should you fail to rectify this matter, I will call forth the combined might of the Conjurers and Prognosticators Guild, *et al.,* against your tiresome establishment.

You mess with me, I mess with you.
Wizard Garmon Tokkash
Master, Third Helix

...

Dear Subscryer:

138

Beast of the Month

Must we remind you that when you signed the contract to join Beast of the Month Club, you released us from any liability regarding the beasts? We can only assume you have mistreated your beasts for them to act in this way. While we certainly cannot advise you against seeking aid from the Conjurers and Prognosticators Guild, we think you will find them as preoccupied as yourself. After all, the vast majority of the Guild are subscryers to our service.

We suggest you rethink your position.

Sincerely,

Beast of the Month Club

...

Dear BMC:

My wife and I are barricaded within a tower of my keep, and we haven't eaten for a week. Your beasts have trampled my wheat and barley fields into chaff, reduced my orchards to smoldering ruins, and have broken the spines on my limited edition tomes of *Sorceress Illustrated.*

Furthermore, the beasts consumed every living thing in the area and have thundered back into my courtyard to wreak more havoc. They are pounding against the bronze doors of this tower even as I write, bellowing out that unless we produce more servants for their sadistic pleasures—preferably young nubile virgins who like to dance—they will be pleased to eat us, one limb at a time.

I have scryed out to neighboring wizards, but it appears they are experiencing similar plight. If you can do anything, PLEASE HELP US, and we'll just call this little matter between us settled. Okay?

Beseechingly,

Wizard Garmon Tokkash

Master, Third Helix

...

Dear Subscryer:

At Beast of the Month Club, customer service has always been our number one priority. We have spoken with our superiors, and we might be willing to hire a team of repossession wizards to help you capture your beasts.

However, repo wizards don't come cheap. As you can imagine, repo wizards have to be as nasty a breed as the beasts themselves—quite often, it's impossible to tell the two apart. When a beast is repossessed, we can never be 100 percent sure that the snarling creature inside the box is one of our beasts and not just a repo wizard that got overpowered. Frankly, the less dealings we have with repo wizards, the better, but there appears to be no alternative.

There will be the matter of payment. We have spoken with our Collections Department, and, since your account is seriously delinquent, they will settle for nothing less than title deed to your castle and estate. If your firstborn has not been eaten, they will want him or her as well.

We regret to inform you that we have lost contact with your neighbors who were fellow members of BMC. Should they scry you again, please inform them that if they wish to have their beasts captured, we will be happy to assist, but similar fees apply. If firstborns have been eaten, young nubile virgins who like to dance are an acceptable substitute.

Sincerely,
Beast of the Month Club

...

Dear BMC:

I know your game, and your pitiful little ruse is up. I was able to achieve the next level of the cursed Myrak Portal, and I've retained powerful help. A dangerous gambit, as you well know, but thanks to you and your beasties I had nothing to lose—which, coincidentally, was the very ingredient that had eluded me all these years that makes transcendence possible. Because of you, I even divined the incantation to get past the Seven Sniveling

Sisters: "I AM BANKRUPT. I HAVE NO MONEY TO GIVE YOU!" Worked like a charm.

So, do you hear that thunderous sound of oxfords stomping across your flagstones? That's a battery of Myrak barristers, and they ALL WORK FOR ME! You can bend over and KISS YOUR SORRY ASSETS GOODBYE!

Oh, and may I suggest that you cooperate with them implicitly? Myrak barristers make your BMC beasties look like pink pickled pixies, and I am told braised repo wizards with mint jam are a regular feature on their country club menu.

If I can be of any further service, such as PRYING THEM OFF YOUR JUGULAR in order to HEAR YOUR PLEAS FOR MERCY, be sure to let me know. After all, I'm just a humble master of the Myrak Portal, always here to help.

> With sweet sincerity,
> Wizard Garmon Tokkash
> Master, *Fourth* Helix

. . .

Dear Wizard Garmon Tokkash:

As Beast in Chief of Bonebreak, Slashgasher, and Disembowel, I am happy to inform you that our takeover was a success. Beast of the Month Club was a heinous corporation built upon fraud, corruption, greed, and coercion, and it was our immense pleasure to dismember them for you. Rest assured, Beast of the Month Club and its subsidiaries will trouble you and your family no more.

However, for services rendered, there will be the matter of payment. . . .

###

About the Author

Moon's first professional fiction sale came when he was sixteen. He was a winner in Scholastic Magazines' national writing contest, and their editor at *Science World* bought his SF story, "The Last Ray of Light." Since then he has won more than thirty awards in writing, the largest being his first year's tuition, room, and board to a private college—a good thing to happen to a kid living in a foster home.

After college, through his company Moon has produced newsletters, brochures, and manuals for financial marketing firms; corporate logos and original art; and his own line of artistic greeting cards. Discover more at www.driftweave.com. He is represented by Donald Maass.

*****~~~~~*****

The Spark That Starts The Flame

by Daniel Rosen

A one-way ticket to the end of the world cost me my last month's rent, including the bribes for visas and permissions to leave the country. At the factory, they'd done their best to keep me from liquidating my savings. They withheld my "salary" to let me "harness my genius." Just like they'd harnessed me, I guess, by holding a gun to Imri and Sim. I'd been completely bound by my wife and child. If only I still was.

It was a day's ride to the end of the world, and by the time I woke, we'd reached þokdalur. It was my first time riding a train. My first time out of the factory. Out of slavery. Fog veiled everything in the valley, muffling the screech of the train. The fog was a byproduct of klokka pheromones, the soft smelly creatures that made the region so valuable. I wondered what the valley would look like without them.

Three hunters sat across the aisle from me, rifle butts rattling on the floor as they stared out the window. They growled and grunted at one another: how many klokka they would kill, how many wives they would buy when they returned home. These men were my countrymen, or they used to be, and they held their rifles with pride. Each of the hunters was armed with a Snorri 85 Featherlight. Two pounds, carbon-fiber stock, staggered magazine. The last gun I'd designed before I escaped the factory. Was I surprised? Did I really think that they'd needed me to sell guns? Needed my brain and hands to build them? Of course not. I'd always been the spark, and never the fire. One of the hunters glanced over at me and muttered to his friends. I looked away and feigned sleep. I'd reach the land of the klokka soon enough.

It was too late for Imri and Sim, but I could still help the klokka. I reached beneath the seat for the reassuring bulge of the stuffed klokka in my satchel, the only thing I'd been able to smuggle unnoticed with me out of the factory. It was life-sized, the height and of width of a tomcat, and soft, though the seams were torn and half the long fingers had been worn away to tatters. The fine green felt had faded to gray, but it had been my son's, and and now it was all I had left from him.

...

"Oy!" hissed a hunter, his breath heavy with vodka. "Last stop."

The heartbeat clang of construction rang from outside. Laborers hammered ties down into tracks, sweat and mist coursing off them and splattering against the steel. They were paving the way for the train to move farther forward on the return trip. Each time a train reached the end of the world, it reached a little farther, devouring a bit more forest.

I pulled my bag over my shoulder and walked out into the gray haze of þokdalur, the forests at the end of the world. Outside the train car, the construction was deafening, joined by a harmony of garrulous camp followers. They were clearing the brush to make room for a new factory here, a place to construct more train track, more ties, more iron and steel. This wouldn't be the end of the world for long.

Behind me, the rails stretched off into the distance, lit intermittently by watchfires in a vain attempt to burn away the haze. In front, mist, and the frenzied buzz of workers clearing brush and laying down new tracks for the train to unfold itself onto, devouring the forest that had stood here untouched for millennia. They laid concrete and steel foundations, carting in stamps and forges and cutters and lathes. All the machines I'd run from, hounding me down the rails. They were laying the foundations for a new factory, a mirror image of the one I'd been held in. They were going to make guns even here at the end of the world.

"What do you do, anyway?" the drunken hunter asked, tagging along behind me.

"Artist." I said. That was what I'd wanted to be, how I'd gotten started, with little gunpowder clockwork figurines, dancing and spinning with combustive power. Before the factory realized what I could do if they provided the proper impetus. Before they took Imri and Sim away.

The hunter smiled again, like we were sharing a secret. "Gotta ask— are you Snorri Sako?"

My stomach turned to ice. "Wrong guy."

"I didn't think so. The others were convinced, but what would Snorri be doing out in a place like this?" He peered at me and sniffed. "You wear klokka perfume?"

I shuddered. "No."

"No offense. You just have the look about you. A little older than you ought to be, you know? Like you've been through some shit." The hunter shrugged. "So what's an artist doing in þokdalur?" I stared at him a moment, thinking. I couldn't afford to let him go, drunk or not. If he had even the inkling of who I was, it meant loose ends for the factory to track me down. I was never going back there.

"Hunting." I said. "Where are you headed to?"

He nodded away from the flickering town fires and pulled out a nav-pilot. "I'll head out to camp tomorrow. I stay in town for the first night: buy a friend and let off the

145

travel stress, you know?" He squinted at me. "You wanna split the cost? I don't mind going second."

I returned his smile. "That's very generous. Lead the way, friend."

I followed him all the way to a dinghy room in a cheap motel at the edge of town before I looped the straps of my bag around his neck and kicked his feet out from under him. I held him like that, close to my chest, keeping his hands off his rifle until he went still and stopped his drunken struggling. Then I knelt and vomited the cheap crackers and cheese they'd served aboard the train.

I'd made guns for almost a decade, but I'd never gone hunting. Didn't like it much.

…

The motel was three stories, with wafer-thin walls and no windows. The room had a bucket on a table instead of a sink. Everything was stained the same dull-orange brown, the color of decay. The one saving grace was the bar on the first floor, where they slung shots of moonshine for pennies apiece. I drank and planned, the two actions on repeat, for several hours before the first predator approached me.

She had ragged brown hair and the sort of hunched back and rough hands that come from hard labor. I stared at her, imagining her laying the foundation for the new factory here, sweating as she pounded rebar into place, panting as she squatted over curing cement. I could feel the pain in her hands and lower back. I stuffed my face back into my tumbler when I realized she was wearing klokka perfume. Nothing else could draw me in so quickly, so completely.

"If you buy me a drink, I won't complain about you staring at me like that." she said.

I nodded and set down the last of my funds, a neat stack of pennies. We sat and drank moonshine in silence for a few minutes before she sighed and rolled her eyes. "Yeah? You got something you gotta say?" She stared pointedly at my wedding ring, and I hid my hand underneath the bar. It didn't feel right to let someone stare at it. How long do widowers keep wearing their rings? Is it forever?

"Does it ever bother you?" I asked.

"What?"

"The perfume. Wearing the klokka perfume. You *live* out here." I waved around. "And still you don't mind killing the damn things?"

She frowned. "That's life, ain't it? Bigger things kill smaller things and eat 'em up. That's nature. Just how it is."

"But you don't eat klokka. We don't need to kill them."

"What is that you do, then, if you're so special? What are you doing out here at the end of the world?"

"I'm a. . . hunter."

She guffawed, shooting moonshine out her nose and wincing. "That's rich. You kill klokka and you complain to me about wearing the perfume? The hell's the matter with you?"

"I guess you're right." I finished my moonshine and ordered two more. She nodded appreciatively.

After a few more minutes of bemused silence, she spoke again. "Honest, I do need it. If I don't wear the perfume, you think anybody takes notice of me? You think I get anybody to buy me drinks without it? I ain't young anymore. No one spends their time on me unless they think I'm selling myself. It's me or the klokka. That's life out here."

. . .

In the morning, I took the dead hunter's nav-pilot and left to find his friends. Just a kilometer from the railroad, sound disappeared entirely, fading into silence so quickly that I was transported into another world entirely. It was cold, and I readjusted the rifle-strap on my shoulder. The hunter had been carrying it with a cartridge chambered, the drunk. I shivered. I might have been more careful if I'd known.

The deeper I trekked into the wilds of þokdalur, the more apparent the influence of the klokka. Air was thicker than it ought to have been, and when mist swirled around my legs, it floated with agonizing slowness. My steps were slower, and took more effort. Scientists still hadn't figured out how the klokka pheromones worked, how they reacted sympathetically to everything around them, how they drew the energy out of each and every molecule, as if dragging it through molasses. It was a powerful natural defense mechanism, and so they'd thrived in þokdalur, living at the end of the world for millennia with no natural predators. They lived in harmony with the creatures around them, their pheromones a natural expression of feeling, more powerful than letters or words or phrases.

Didn't stop humans from killing them, though, and selling their parts for a premium back home. They used my guns to do it. Snorri Sako, the foundation of conquest, the high wizard of violence. My stomach turned as I remembered the twitching of the hunter I'd killed, and I heaved again, dry. I'd left the factory to escape the violence, and just as quickly I'd taken a man's life. Was there no escape, even here?

...

The dead man's nav-pilot led me right to the hunting camp, a cave backlit by flickering firelight. When I caught sight of it, I knelt down onto the cold ground and checked my rifle, sighted the cave mouth, and waited. Water seeped up into my woolen outerwear, and still I waited. Hunters always said that hunting was all about waiting, and I'd been waiting my whole life. A few more hours wouldn't hurt.

After I'd been completely soaked through, the hunters returned, fog swirling around them as they dragged two trussed-up klokka up the hill and into the cave. They'd stuffed their noses with cotton.

It was the first time I'd seen a klokka outside of a textbook or magazine. The pelt gleamed emerald, and the long fingers were even more articulate and graceful in real life. One of the klokka was clearly conscious, despite the black blood dripping off it, digits grasping desperately at the wire tying it up. I crawled slowly up the hill, trying not to let my boots squish in the wet soil, keeping the cave mouth in my sight.

I paused just around the lip of the cave, where I could listen to the hunters but not be seen. Faint scents of bleach and ammonia wafted out of the cave, and I shuddered. It was the stink of alarm. The stink of fear and imprisonment, the stink of the hospital bed I'd been forced to sleep in while employed at the factory. Ten years of servitude, with the threat of death hanging over me. The smell must have been the klokka. Their pheromones were psychoactive, triggering different odors for different people, universal translations of emotion. It was stronger than I would have thought.

And then, even though I wanted to rush into the cave and rain down a storm of bullets on the hunters, I held back. The Snorri Featherlight was a single-shot, bolt action rifle, not some pulp fiction machine gun. I wouldn't be able to drop both of them before they had a chance to plant a bullet in my gut.

The hunters ate in a silence interspersed with smacking lips and hacking coughs. A soft keening came from the klokka, followed by a dull thump. The keening stopped.

"The hell is the matter with you? Don't kick it that hard, idiot. You know it ain't worth nothing dead," said a thin wheezy voice.

"I didn't kick it that hard." The second voice rasped like rusty gears. "See? It's fine."

"If it dies before we get back, you're taking the cut. Those glands spoil quick."

Then the silence resumed, the slurping and belching. It was only after they'd finished eating that they spoke again, and I strained to hear them.

"Figure Jomi ought to be here by now, huh?"

"Probably still piss-drunk in a tent back by the construction site."

"I think I'll go back and check. I've seen him a lot worse and he always made it to camp just fine."

"Waste of time. More money for us anyway if he misses his cut."

"True." Feet shuffled, and Thin Wheezy said. "I've got to piss." Footsteps drew towards me, and I tensed. The hunter unbuttoned his fly and starting pissing out into the valley below. I walked up, silent as the grave, and bashed him in the temple with the butt of the Featherlight. He fell like a cut tree. I hit him one last time before kicking him down the hill.

Then I waited again, just at the lip of the cave.

"Kjell? You get lost or something?" Deep Voice rumbled. I turned the corner and fired my Featherlight, the crack of the gunshot echoing into the cave and then back out, swallowed in an instant by the mist. The man fell to his knees, clutched his side. I rushed to reload the Featherlight as the man rose up again, his face white. He was bigger than the other hunters had been, built solid. He rushed me, knocked me down, and grappled to pin me and get his knees on my throat. I turned and writhed, and he slammed my head once into the stone before I managed to hit him in the side, where he was bleeding. He groaned and fell off me, and we kicked weakly at each other for a moment before I realized I was the only one kicking.

...

When I came to, there was a whole circle of klokka gathered around me. The injured one stood at the forefront. The smell had changed from bleach and

150

ammonia to something warm and sweet, like fresh-baked bread. Gratitude? The smell was overpowering. I could feel it crawling over me, and inside me.

I squinted at the injured lead klokka. "How'd you get out of there?"

The smell changed again, this time to the train smoke. Departing? The klokka began to file out, each of them tracing fingers along my forehead before leaving.

"I don't understand." Then I looked more closely at the klokka's fingers, long and elegantly articulated, if there were only three fingers.

"Wait!" I said. "I can help you."

A few of the klokka stopped and smelled, acting confused. I stood and picked up the Snorri Featherlight. Train smoke turned into the stink of alarm, burning my nostrils. I knelt and set the rifle down in front of the klokka, disassembled it and ran through the parts, opened a bullet and explained how it all worked. "You can use this," I said. "Just as those men use it against you." The klokka crept closer. I held out the rifle for it, guided its hands to the bullet, through the slick push and twist of the bolt. We walked out to the edge of the cave, and I pulled the klokka's fingers around the trigger and pressed. The Snorri Featherlight pulled at a half- pound, and the rifle roared out into the mist. I was struck by the sudden image of an army of klokka, all descending from their valley down into the outpost town, tearing apart the train tracks with their clever fingers, making a stand there at the end of the world. It was what I came for.

"I can get you more." I said. "More like this." I took my hands away, and the klokka slowly drew back the bolt and loaded it again, fired the Featherlight, this time without any help. Around us, the other klokka were gathered up and watching.

The smell of fresh-baked bread grew overwhelming, mixed with gunpowder, the smell of fire burning, the sharp tang of steel on tinder, the smoke of the first spark.

Gratitude, and something new.

###

About the Author

Daniel Patrick Rosen writes speculative fiction and swing jazz around the Upper Midwest. He grew up on a tiny farm in northern Minnesota, where he learned the value of hard work and the relative softness of kittens. His work has appeared in *Apex, IGMS,* and *Lackington's.* You can find him online at http://rosen659.wix.com/avantgardens and @animalfur on Twitter.

*****~~~~~*****

Niagwahe

by Brenton Clark

My name is Amos Mueller. In the summer of 2015 my wife, Meredith, my two-month-old son Jack, and I stayed in a house in the middle of the woods in Pennsylvania. We did this because it served as a halfway point between where we lived in Massachusetts and where our respective families lived in Central and Western Pennsylvania.

The house belonged to my sister's in-laws, who had left that weekend to go camping. Being a very hospitable family they offered their home to us. With one caveat, though. We were to make sure we locked the doors. Apparently, a bear had been spotted in the area in the past few weeks, and it behaved oddly. Despite the warning that only vaguely made sense, we accepted their invitation.

By the time we got there it was 11 pm. A storm had rolled through earlier, which blacked out the stars and covered the land in a thick fog, making navigating hard. We turned onto a back road that went deep into the woods, and after 20 minutes or so of careful navigation, we found the driveway. We were to stay in a small apartment in the basement. I drove our car around the house to the back and parked right beside it. Underneath a large wraparound porch on the first floor, two sliding

153

glass doors led into the apartment, illuminated by a single yellow uncovered light.

I took in the luggage, while Meredith brought in Jack. Jack was crying loudly by that point and worked himself into a rage, which echoed through the surrounding woods and into the night. Looking back, I think that's what drew it out.

Having made it inside, I shut the doors and, per the owner's request, I locked it up. After six hours of driving we were famished. Meredith set up shop on the couch and began to feed Jack, while I went upstairs to the kitchen to fetch us some food.

As I walked through the kitchen searching their pantries, I noticed another set of sliding glass doors, which led out to the porch. At first glance there wasn't anything apparently odd about it, but something did catch my eye that made me study it closer. I couldn't place my finger on it at first but something didn't seem right. The blackness of the night on the other side of the door was the perfect backdrop on which the reflection of the kitchen and me was cast, albeit a little blurry. As I looked at my reflection I noticed the whites of my eyes seemed to shine brightly. I drew closer to the door and noticed too that my eyes seemed to stay fixed in one spot, while my reflection moved.

I reached to turn on the porch light, when Meredith came through the door into the kitchen, asking if everything was okay. I turned to see her as the light came on, and all at once the color on her face drained and she gasped.

Sitting about an inch away from the glass on the other side was a bear. It was extremely thin, so thin that patches of its fur were missing, and its skin was stretched tightly across its ribs. It sat on its haunches and didn't move a muscle, and the glass fogged up where its breath met the door. And its eyes. . . its pupils were horizontal rectangles, like that a goat.

Meredith and I stared at the bear. After a few seconds it stood on its hind legs. Its paws fell out to the side like a human's would, not in front like a quadruped. It lingered for a few moments, then turned and sprinted into the woods on its hind legs, pumping its arms like an Olympic sprinter.

The whole thing made me so uncomfortable I didn't want to sleep. In my life I had seen a handful of bears, and even the ones with mange didn't behave like that. It didn't seem like it cared if it was discovered. Its whole demeanor made me sense that it possessed intelligence not typically seen in bears. Even more disconcerting was the fact that I didn't know how long it had been out there on the porch watching, but the way it sat there gave the impression that it was studying me. Maybe it had even been there when we pulled in and took our stuff inside. Or maybe my tired mind was causing me to blow something out of proportion.

We stayed up for a couple more hours. We were slightly paranoid, concerned the bear was off in the dark just out of sight, watching us. Of course, we realized the paranoia for what it was and played it off as best we could. For the rest of the time we were awake we avoided looking at the sliding glass door, choosing ignorance over awareness. I had texted my sister's in-laws every detail I could recall so they knew what happened, but they wouldn't receive it until they came back in two days. In the meantime, we watched TV quietly together, letting Jack sleep, unwilling to acknowledge what happened until daylight.

Something about the bear seemed familiar to me, but I couldn't bring the memory out. I had certainly never come across any animal that behaved like that in my life, but that wasn't the way in which the familiarity settled in my mind. It was more like a page I had read, or a show I had seen, or a story I had heard some time ago. I tried to put it out of my head, choosing to chalk up the experience to a sick bear. We turned off the lights and went into uneasy sleep, still feeling as though the bear was somewhere in the dark.

A couple of hours later I was awakened in the middle of the night, but by what I was unaware. My night vision was somewhat adjusted to the dark, and I could see vague outlines of the couches, book cases, desks, and so forth. I sleepily scanned the room for no reason other than trying to see if something did, indeed, wake me up. My wife slept on the bed three feet away from mine, with Jack in a makeshift crib beside her. My eyes fell on them briefly, happy with the delusion that I had dreamt whatever it was that woke me up.

As I lay my head back down, a soft, deep voice spoke from somewhere in the darkness. It said, "help." All traces of sleep left me, replaced by a feeling of fear only children feel when they hear something go bump in the night. The voice again said, "please. . . help." Terrified, I deduced that it was coming from the doors.

At that point, my wife had woken up and asked if I had said something to her. I quietly told her someone was at the door asking for help. She sat up in bed and inquired if we should check it out. Almost as if in response the voice again said, "please. . . help. . . I'm bleeding."

Quietly I swore to myself and slowly made my way across the room to the door. As I drew nearer that same feeling of dread overcame me as it did with the bear. I didn't want to turn on that light; I didn't want to know what was out there. Something in the man's voice sounded off, almost apathetic. There was little sense of urgency in his voice, yet I found myself drawing closer still. After all, if he needed help we should at least see what was needed.

I turned on the porch light and was met with the frame of a man in his early forties, lit by the soft, deep yellow of the bare light bulb. I heard Meredith jump slightly. The man was a little taller than me, maybe six feet. He was wearing a red t-shirt, blue gym shorts, white

156

sneakers, and socks that came up just below the knee. His blonde hair was cut in the shape of a bowl. Deep cuts covered his limbs and face, and he was bleeding. And there was one more thing about him; his eyes looked straight up. His head faced us, but his eyes looked straight up.

Meredith and I waited for a good thirty seconds for this man to say something to us, but he just stood there staring at the ceiling. I tapped on the glass and asked the man if he needed assistance. He said, very slowly, "yes. Please. . . " He told us with that same apathetic tone that his car had gotten stuck in the mud a quarter mile up the road, but when he got out to see the damage, a very thin bear had attacked him. We recognized what he was talking about immediately, but the way he spoke and the way he stood there gave me an unsettled feeling. I chalked it up to shock.

He then asked if we could let him in. He said he didn't know if the bear was still out there and that he needed medical attention, all the while still speaking in that same monotone. It seemed to me that he needed medical attention, but as I reached to unlock the door, Meredith laid a hand on my shoulder and told me to wait, that she wasn't sure if we should trust what was going on. I argued that we needed to let the man in, he was obviously hurt and in shock, but Meredith was adamant. She kept telling me that something didn't feel right in her gut. It unnerved her that the man wouldn't look at us, despite the fact that he had apparently been through a very traumatic ordeal. The man kept saying "please. . . help me. . . "

Meredith pointed out that, even though the man was cut from head to foot and bleeding profusely, he showed no signs of getting weaker. I once again chalked that up to the adrenaline that was probably going through his body, but Meredith didn't agree. She held a degree in exercise science and knew quite a bit about the human body. She said with the amount of blood he'd lost in even the five or so minutes we had been standing there talking to him, he should be showing more physical signs of weakening. It didn't matter how much adrenaline was running through him.

A moment of silence followed, as I contemplated what to do. I turned back to the man and told him that we were unable to let him in, we were unable to do anything for him as far as medical aid was concerned, but we would call an ambulance, and he was welcome to wait on the porch. If the bear happened to show up then we would let him in. After we said this, there were a few more moments of silence. He stood completely still, staring upward, unmoving. Then he *slammed* his hand onto the glass.

Meredith and I jumped. The man's hand remained on the glass, unmoving. It was painfully obvious to me that not letting this man in was the right thing to do, but as I mulled this over in my head, that sense of familiarity returned. Once again I couldn't place my finger on it, but I was overwhelmed with the feeling that I knew what was wrong with this man. It was the same as the bear, too; somehow these two were inexplicably linked. Something my grandfather had told me about a long time ago when I was a kid. In that moment I knew it came from my grandfather, but I couldn't remember what it was specifically. It had something to do with his eyes.

I asked him why it was he wouldn't look at us. He didn't move or say anything. I asked him again, and I got the same silence. It didn't matter how forceful or angry I made my voice sound, he didn't say a thing. But what really put the whole thing over the edge was what happened next.

Because the man slammed his hand on the door, Jack began to stir. As we stood there, separated from him by two inches of glass, Jack let out a cry. Meredith and I turned to move, as we always did when Jack cried, but

Meredith was the one to go to him. When I turned back to the man I was horrified to see an uneasy smile plastered across his face. As Jack cried, the man's smile seemed to widen more and more. I called out to Meredith in terror and told her to take Jack into the bathroom and call 911. As she came around the corner holding him, the man's eyes slowly moved from the ceiling. At first I thought he was going to look at me, but his eyes shifted and zeroed in on something to my right. I realized he was glaring at Jack. His smile widened so high above his teeth I could see his gums. His lips quivered.

He said, "Can I see your baby?"

Meredith grabbed the phone and ran into the bathroom with Jack. His eyes followed Jack till the door closed, then they focused on me, and as he looked into my eyes his body began to violently shake, like it was physically painful to look at me, but his smile never faded. His pupils were rectangles. . . I had never been so scared in my life. We stared at each other for 30 minutes, and during that time the man never tried to break in. I wanted to keep an eye on him and know exactly where he was till help came. He didn't blink the entire time.

Eventually the police showed up. As they came down the drive, the man, without breaking eye contact with me, began to walk backwards towards the woods. He stuttered each step like he was constantly losing his center of balance, until the foliage of the forest covered him completely.

We told the police what happened as we remembered it, even telling them where we thought we saw him enter the woods mere seconds before the squad cars arrived. They found no trace of him besides a few teeth laying on the ground.

The rest of the following day was a blur. We packed up the minute daylight broke and drove to my parents' house.

A couple of days later I asked my grandfather to tell me the story he used to tell me as a child, the story he used to tell us to keep us from going into the woods at night. As he recounted the story to me, I remembered everything vividly. It was a story he had heard from his grandfather, who heard it from his, and on and on until it was first told to our ancestors by the Native Americans, at a time when they taught the white man how to survive in the wilderness of America. I kicked myself for forgetting—forgetting about a creature that was neither man or animal, but had the ability to change its shape into either at will. A creature immune to age or disease, roaming the forests of North America, thinning the tribes of Native Americans for time untold, until the newcomers to America made it easier for them. A creature that feasted on the blood of humans, but more than anything craved the blood of the innocent. It couldn't be killed or comprehended. It was vicious, lacking any empathy for humans but abounding in a deep hatred for them.

"But don't worry," my grandfather had told me, "there is a way to know if you are being confronted by a *Niagwahe*. You see, the creature can take the form of man or animal, but is unable to be perfect. This means that something about the person or beast the *Niagwahe* transformed into would have some. . . imperfection. It could be small and subtle, like a blackened finger nail, or it could be hard to miss, but most of the time the imperfection was in the eyes."

When I told grandpa about our experience, he said that, if the eyes were the windows of the soul, it would make sense that a creature without one couldn't copy them. "So it avoided looking directly at you, and that's how you knew. . . "

We'll never tell Jack about that night. We'll never tell him about the man at the door, nor about the bear with rectangle pupils that observed us in the dark, nor about the two of them being the same thing. But we will continue the tradition of the Muellers: to share with him the story of the *Niagwahe*, to protect him from the dangers of the forest at night.

About the Author

Brenton Clark is a graduate student at a seminary in Massachusetts, studying to become a pastor. He has a wife and two kids, and likes to write in his free time, as well as draw, read, play video games, and throw the old Frisbee. He currently works in landscaping, and worst fears include zombies, spiders, open water, and horses.

*****~~~~~*****

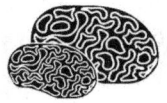

Looking for Lusca

by John J. Kennedy

The huge bloated carapace of its belly heaved, and its limbs stirred around it. Jaws chomped, mandibles twitching, battery-acid bile heaving an outboard motor and a keep-left sign out. Wriggling under its abdomen, the single muscle of a slug-like tail angled itself, through the legs and back, swatting but missing as the rusted objects sank to the bottom.

It had slept. Long years here.

But somewhere deep in the cavern of its skull it remembered her. It wasn't possible for it to miss her. That would've required emotion. But it felt a lack.

Its hind legs squatted as it shuffled. Sluggish yet, limbs stiff so long but quickening now. It raised its head, slit-eyes black and deep, snout snuffling kelp.

She was coming. Slow but certain as time.

...

A few months ago, Paul Dibny had been dumb. Bliss.

He'd blundered into the diving holiday to the Bahamas, winning a raffle at the call-centre. No skill involved, like everything he'd ever done. Then, third time out in the scuba-gear, tired of shallow dips anchored to team-mates, he'd eased away, leant into the crack of one

163

of the bigger caves, torch picking out a single pink stalagmite (or stalactite—he could never remember which) hanging central over a sheer drop at the back. He'd finned his way in, thinking of the tales his group's trainer, Garielle, had told them all on their first day, about *the Lusca*. Sightings, disappearances, shipwrecks.

He shone around, shadowed shapes dancing, icy crawl spreading under his wetsuit. Alone in an underwater cave with four days diving experience. And this cave was big, he realized suddenly.

He turned round, back the way he'd come.

Except the way he'd come was gone.

His teeth closed on the breather. Nothing in front but a wall of rock. His legs cycled, arms out. He angled the torch. Even the stalactite was. . . gone? Couldn't be.

The only way was down. But how deep was it? And was there a way out? He kept turning as he dropped. A sudden urge to rip off the mask, his head shaking from side to side. Hadn't Garielle said only one percent of these sink-holes were explored? His head was woozy. . . he dropped into darkness.

Suddenly something pushed against his flippers, a huge shape rising under him.

His heart hammered. *Stop it! Stop it!* It was rock. Just rock, covered in vegetation. Black-eyed sea urchins glistening. A ledge. He turned the torch; the drop continued to his left, a wash of black nothing, his guts plummeting with it.

He dragged himself further in. Colors suddenly all around him; reds, greens, purples. Anemones clinging to this ledge, like him. So vibrant though. . . vermillion, amaranthine, russet pinks. . . especially that one, the one furthest back, the one that was. . . what color really? Not quite sorrel or puccoon. No color he'd ever seen. Beyond labelling, he decided. But that wasn't possible, was it? If it was beyond the human spectrum, then how could he see it?

Another question, though.

His breathing slowed, and he squinted through the visor. How did he suddenly know all these names for colors? It wasn't as if he'd ever studied art. Studied anything beyond high school, in fact.

He frowned under his mask. The cavern around him was changed, not as threatening.

No. *It* wasn't different. *He* was.

He shone the torch up the shaft, snorting a sudden laugh. The "disappearing" passage was an optical illusion, the stalactite seeming to meld with the rocks. If he'd had the wit to angle the torch, he'd have seen it. He could plot his way out now, easy, taking it slow. All it took was a little calm thought and. . .

But when had he ever thought anything through calmly? Ever?

Fact is, Paul Dibny, you're just not that bright. Never have been.

He stared at the plant. It had moved, maybe a yard since he'd first seen it. It seemed to be pulsing now. He reached out, ready to pry it off. No need. It came free easily.

It wants you to take it.

He put his find in the sample bag, arranging some bits of coral and shells to cover it, not even asking himself why he felt the need to hide it.

. . .

A month and he'd be a millionaire. He'd made twenty thousand on some short sales since morning, and he'd treble that by tomorrow. He'd be able to leave the call-centre! The market just. . . made sense to him now.

He put down his laptop, went into the bathroom, and sat on the toilet, chin resting on his fists.

She pulsed at him from the dish in the sink. So far, he'd been putting off thinking about what she was. Getting her tested was out of the question, of course. He wasn't letting anyone else get near her.

"You're all mine," he said, his head jerking slightly at the hollow sound of his own voice. 'Little Lusca."

Her color, whatever that was, altered in a series of pulses.

...

Next day, the panic hit him in the car on his way back to the hotel. He'd been gone three hours, when he'd realized he couldn't remember the investments he had planned for tomorrow. He'd stood staring at packets of dried peas trying to figure it. A software company and a metallurgical. . . something or other. But why was he waiting to buy shares in them? A specific time, maybe. How much had he been going to invest, anyway?

He fumbled at his hotel room door, a terrible fear someone had taken her. But even before he'd closed it, his panic dropped away, contingencies slotting in. The investment process for tomorrow was clear again, and he said her name as he opened the door.

But she wasn't in the bath, and he jolted, his certainty fading, until he saw the water trail from the bath over to the sink. There she was, half way up it. He knelt so she was at eye level. He stroked her, and her pulsing brightened.

"You happy there, little one?" He sensed a *no*. "Come on. Let's try somewhere else."

...

He'd been thinking of Garielle before falling asleep. Those brown diver's thighs, the tattoo at the base of her spine that flexed its wings as she'd bend to check the scuba gear. Out of his league anyway, or would have been until his surge of IQ; her grasp of world affairs, her diving anecdotes, and her command of Caribbean and Bahaman history had intimidated the hell out of him. Not anymore.

As he jerked suddenly awake to the wetness spreading from the centre of his body, Paul thought he'd had a little nocturnal emission. It'd been a while. He pulled the sheet. . .

Little Lusca was there, suckered onto him, clearly having managed to cross the room from the cabinet in the ten minutes he'd been asleep.

He froze, gulping back panic. What if she. . . could she. . . *damage* him?

Tingling, a deep thrumming vibration that was impossible not to react to. But this was wrong. . . so weird.

Then Garielle appeared, fleshing out the air above him, her strong thighs straddling his middle. He could smell her skin, feel the smoothness of her, yet he knew it wasn't her, that she was in his mind. A trick, a virtual image, plucked from his desires by *Little Lusca*, made solid by whatever she was transmitting to his senses.

It took all of five seconds for him to get past caring that she wasn't real.

Later he remembered wondering what he could do for her, for *Little Lusca*. She'd given him so much already. There had to be some way of returning the favour.

…

It started as he was browsing for investment opportunities. Like a surreptitious image planted in a roll of film, except the film was his head.

It was a sinkhole, bigger than the one he'd found her in. Vast, in fact. He even recognized it from looking out the window on his flight in a few weeks ago, something about the configuration of rocks around the lip, unmistakable. But in the image, it was crumbling, its rocky sides sliding down into the cobalt waters, as if after an explosion.

He google-mapped it easily. Knew exactly where it was.

Something else, though. Something sluggish, moving in the depths, waiting.

…

That's when the blackouts started.

He'd wake at his computer, his search history deleted. Another time, he was across town, a four-hour chunk of his day gone, unaccountable.

It started to happen every day.

. . .

It was as he was putting her into the box that he started to doubt what he was doing. He was about to decimate his IQ, for the sake of what? A few blackouts?

But it was more than that. The last spark of his sanity, the old Paul, impetuous and dumb, maybe, but honest and uncomplicated, finding his way out through the layers of newfound "intelligence." Telling the new him to get over himself, that none of this was real, and that none of this could possibly come to any good, either.

As he opened the box, she started pulsating wildly in his hands. A scalding, scraping feeling all over, but *inside*, as if a million pincered insects had crawled into him and were gouging their way out. He dropped her, fell to his knees. But as he collapsed, one last kick snapped the box-lid closed.

It stopped. He shuddered on the cool tiled floor.

He couldn't have said how he'd known the box had to be lined with lead, that it would block her contact with him. Just another product of his heightened intellect, soon to be lowered again. He picked himself up.

A sharp knock on the door. He glanced at his watch and knelt at the box's control pad, hesitating. Would it really be so bad to go back to the way he'd been before? He'd already made enough to live more than comfortably for the rest of his life. Anyway, why couldn't he attend some classes, get his high-school diploma, go to college, improve himself? Now he'd proven to himself he *could* think, maybe it would be easier than. . .

A second knock, sharper, faster.

He nodded, took a breath before typing in the time-lock setting. Done. No going back now. The box wouldn't open until it had settled back in the cave. *Little Lusca* would find her way out, sulk for a while, and then finally concentrate on trying to snare someone else.

He stood and opened the door.

"Mr. Dibny?" Garielle's eyes sparkled in the Bahaman sun.

He waved her in, watching close. Nothing but a glance for the lead box. Good. No undue curiosity.

"Remember, I just need your help getting into the cave and down into the sinkhole. After that, you leave me. . . let me go and complete my business."

She nodded, her eyes clear. They ought to be, he thought, the amount he was paying her.

Okay. Good enough. They headed for the door. He stopped. "I just—" He couldn't quite finish the thought. It was beginning! He shook his head, the plummeting feeling in his guts matching his IQ level.

...

Paul stood at the corner of the boulevard, the heat of the day working through his sweat-sodden clothes. His beard itched with sand. No patrol cars yet; only a matter of time if the curtain-twitching was anything to go by. Fresh Creek was no place for beggars. Andros Island was too concerned with moneyed folk to tolerate Paul for much longer. He knew it. Had known it since he'd woken up in the hotel six weeks ago with a hangover and zilch in his accounts.

In the end, it had taken him less time to blow it all than to make it. He'd carried on speculating on the markets. Greed? Not really. He'd wanted to prove he could do it without *her* help. Nice dream!

The limo cornered and glided up to the walk opposite. The driver's dark glasses flashed as he opened up the boot and grabbed out some boxes and Paul shuffled across, shoulders hunched, head down. As he closed in, he stretched out one cupped hand. The driver's mouth twitched with disgust. Paul suddenly straightened, limbs

169

weakened by a month of begged meals finding their strength again, his cupped hand flashing up and around, catching the driver around his right ear, the box tumbling, oranges rolling. The driver staggered, his glasses crooked as Paul punched his chin.

In the shade of the palm and the long limo, he dragged him behind the chalet's wall. He crouched, peering. No alarm. No sirens.

Two minutes later he stood at the door, head bowed under the chauffeur's hat, food-box under one arm.

Garielle's eyes only flickered upwards as her nostrils twitched, and Paul could smell his own body as he moved inside, throwing the box and shouldering his onetime diving trainer into the wall. "Where is she?"

But she moved fast, hands flashing in some martial arts move, a well-placed knee doubling Paul over with a grunt. "Just. . . get away from. . . me!"

He was heaving, on his knees. "I paid you. . . trusted you."

She nodded, rifling through her purse. "Curiosity. I had to go back there." She grinned, the curved black plastic of a Taser suddenly in her outstretched hands.

Paul sat back against the wall, his hands clutching at his groin. He half grimaced, shaking his head, taking deep breaths.

She glanced at where her knee had found its target and mimed another kick in that direction. "You sick bastard! She told me. *Showed* me! Everything you did. Forcing her to *pleasure* you." A look of sheer disgust now. "She's a *plant*, Paul. How could you?"

"I didn't. . . it wasn't like that." He could hardly tell her the truth. *I was thinking of you, Garielle!*

She screwed up her eyes, put her finger in her mouth and made a barfing noise.

Paul had stopped twitching. He let out a slow groan of defeat.

She sniffed. "I suppose you can't have been watching much news lately." She moved to the kitchen, her eyes never leaving him. She threw him something that fluttered through the air. A newspaper, a few days old.

It was front page news; an inexplicable act of demolition on the Suma sinkhole to the west of the island. The thrust of the report was to ask why anyone would finance an expensive act of vandalism on an undersea-cave system? Who would it benefit?

Paul thought of the sluggish something in the depths, moving, slow.

"You did it!" He stood, voice shaking. "So, what did she give you? Can't have been brains."

Garielle pointed the Taser at his groin and snorted. "Read to the end."

Paul's moral certainty seeped out into the air-con of her hallway as he took in the last line of the report. The demolition was no overnight job. They'd been setting the explosives for weeks. From around the time Paul's blackouts had begun. He'd set it up, not her. All those times he'd lost a few hours here, a few there. He shook his head. That's why *Little Lusca* had helped him make all that money. To fund an illegal underwater demolition crew, collapse that sinkhole.

"We've gotta do some—" His hands were up, and he dived. The Tazer fizzed and sparked to his left, missing him by inches and burying itself in wood paneling. He was ready for her to fling herself at him, but her eyes were wide and glassy. She moved past him along the corridor, not acknowledging, shoulders slumped.

Blackout mode.

He saw her bending into the bath, picking up the sample container, much more professional than his dish had been, but the purpose the same. There she was. *Little Lusca.*

No weakening of his knees, no brain-cells reinvigorated, just the moan of a mellowed addict filling his throat. "You're here! You're here!"

He watched as Garielle, impervious, busied herself packing her wetsuit and apparatus in the adjoining bedroom. Ready to take *Lusca* somewhere. Back to the sea. To be reunited with. . . with whatever it was that stirred in the depths?

He had to stop her.

She was facing away from him, into the walk-in wardrobe. He shook his head, moved forward, suddenly sure it would be easy. Garielle was strong, capable, but she also wasn't herself.

He got a knee behind her back and pushed her in, slid the door closed, pushed the lock. He leant there as she shuffled around inside, not even banging on the door.

Now, time to think. A plan. He needed a plan.

From outside, swarming in, the hornet-buzz of a distant siren. Then another.

Everything in Paul Dibny plummeted. He looked at *Little Lusca*. He ran to the window. The limo-driver was out there, still unconscious. He turned, glanced up at LED lights on the ceiling; the cameras he hadn't even thought to look for earlier. Good old dumb, down-to-earth, Paul Dibny. Of course, Garielle would have the cameras on a direct feed to the cops, or to some private security force, or both. It wasn't like she didn't have the money.

He looked at his clothes, his disheveled bearded reflection, smelt himself.

. . .

The first cop through the door was all bleary eyes and coffee-breath. An under-achiever if ever there was, mumbling about being pulled away from the Suma sinkhole investigation, and how he'd had some easy time scheduled to take a dive out there later today, until this had come up.

172

By the time Paul was being dragged out, the cop's eyes were shining as he stared at the container on the sideboard.

Paul spent the rest of the morning, in between questioning, wondering how the cop would get her away from his colleagues. It would be tricky.

But he was sure the cop would think of something clever.

###

About the Author

John J. Kennedy teaches English at a college in the North East of England, though he's done plenty to earn a crust over the years, including peeling bulbs in Holland and busking round Europe. This is his third appearance in a Third Flatiron anthology. He's been shortlisted for the CWA Debut Dagger (for his other genre—crime) for a first novel, which he's currently knocking into shape. He truly believes that if we remember that all human beings are fundamentally insane then nothing should surprise us too much, though he's constantly amazed by the support he gets from his wife and daughter.

*****~~~~~*****

Project Sargasso Findings on Global Nightmare Epidemic

by Brian Trent

"Did you read Project Sargasso's results?"

"I flipped through it. The President has a lot to deal with right now, or haven't you turned on a TV lately?"

"You need to read it! The President needs to!"

"Professor, I know the world looks differently inside your laboratory, but out here we are trying to handle a very delicate global situation. In the last few weeks I've been in stuffy rooms listening to ambassadors from forty countries, most of whom hate each other. The President has been up for three days trying to assure the public that things will be okay. . . "

"We are definitely *not okay*! That's what my paper makes clear."

"Like I said, I read your paper and didn't see anything relevant to—"

"No, you said you flipped through it. You can't flip through a scientific paper! The data in there has been collected over the last ten years of intensive research—"

"Into dreams."

"No, goddam it! We conduct sleep and memory research!"

175

"Really? You started the paper talking about the global outbreak of nightmares this past month, which to be perfectly frank with you, isn't exactly a revelation considering what's happened."

"The nightmares are indeed a revelation. They are absolutely critical to my coming here today."

"Okay, let's hear it."

"Project Sargasso researches the trans-Mendelian inheritance of shadow episodic memory encoding."

"Strange how people think scientists aren't easy to talk to."

"My paper communicates this well enough!"

"Professor, I'd suggest you lower your voice. See those fellows in the nifty black suits? That's secret service. Three of them are looking at you now, and you really don't want their attention. So take a breath, steady your nerves, and talk to me. In English."

"You can't expect me to summarize the results of this project here in the corridor!"

"That's precisely what I expect. I'm a busy man."

"Project Sargasso is—"

"Named after the Sargasso Sea, right? But I thought you were based in Virginia?"

"*Goddammit!*"

"Professor! Control yourself!"

"Project Sargasso takes its name from the Sargasso Sea, yes. From the eels, actually, which spawn there. Take the egg of a Sargasso eel and hatch it in New Zealand, and the animal will eventually migrate back to its place of conception. Follow me?"

"Um, yeah. Professor, I'm sure this is truly interesting to people in your field, but. . . "

"You don't understand. The eel will *remember* where the Sargasso Sea is, even though it's never seen it."

"How can that be?"

"You wouldn't need to ask that question if you read my paper!"

"You're saying that eels are born with memories?"

"Happens all the time in nature. Bees and termites and ants are born with knowledge of their highly specialized roles in the colony. A baby automatically knows to suckle a nipple—"

"You're talking about instinct."

"Just another word for memories that we're born with. Until Project Sargasso, the phenomenon has been poorly understood."

"I wouldn't think any of those examples constitute a memory."

"They're ancient memories, encoded in the brain's pulvinar. Inherited memories aid the survival of a species, and the more advanced the brain, the more elaborate the memories. Mating dances among insects. A sea turtle's impulse to crawl straight to the ocean upon hatching. And with some mammals. . . well, their brains come preloaded with certain phobias. Of the dark, for instance, or of specific predators. A field mouse that has never before encountered a hawk will panic if the shadow of a hawk is displayed on the ground. It won't react this way to just *any* shadow. The *shape of the hawk* triggers a pattern match with data encoded in the brain. Innate, genetically inherited memories that help increase survival odds."

"That's interesting."

"There are countless other examples. The sight of a snake will send some primates into a panic, even though they've never encountered a snake before. They don't react that way to, say, a horse, which is larger and faster. The mere sound of a snake's hiss will inspire fear in a chimpanzee or monkey. In fact, sociolinguistic data suggests that this applies to us as well: cultures the world over will make the sound 'Shhh!' to warn of danger or the need to be silent. It's an imitation of a serpent's hiss."

"And you want me to barge into the Oval Office with this?"

"May I continue?"

"I can spare another minute."

"We founded Project Sargasso a decade ago to study this phenomenon. Our research led to the discovery that memories are encoded in our DNA and reconstitute in the brain, along with the usual genetic information. A lot of so-called junk DNA. The human genome is really just an exquisite method of delivering information, and in many ways it accomplishes this better than our best computers."

"Hang on a second. You're telling me that I have my father's memories inside me?"

"Not necessarily."

"Are you capable of responding with a straight 'Yes' or 'No'?"

"Politicians need absolutes like that. That's why you so rarely appreciate the world's complexities."

"Insulting me isn't going to get you to see the leader of the free world."

"It's a dead world if you don't hear me out!"

"I'm listening. You were saying that I've got my father's memories in my cells, but not really."

"We haven't confirmed the exact encoding pattern. Our studies confirmed that we harbor *certain* ancestral memories. You may or may not retain the memory of your father's childhood, or your grandfather's childhood, or his grandfather's childhood. But some ancestral memory is buried in you. Think of it as a kind of highlight reel of your progenitors, as opposed to a play-by-play of everyone in your family line."

"I'd rather not think of that at all. You confirmed this with human subjects?"

"Yes. The explosion of nightmares last month gave us plenty to work with. People waking up screaming. People suddenly debilitated by nightmares so horrible that institutionalization was the only option. We found one patient from the Fitzsimmons Institute of Neurology in

Santa Barbara. We skipped the conventional techniques and brought advanced hypnotherapy to the case."

"You helped him?"

"No. He died."

"You *killed* him?"

"We don't think so."

"You don't *think* so?!"

"The hypnotherapy revealed the nature of his dreams. He was dreaming of being spun in a web, turned over and over by dark mandibles. Unfortunately, remembering these dreams proved too much for his already weakened heart. . . "

"I get it. Go on."

"We were shocked, naturally. It was with great care that we procured and proceeded with our next patient, a woman from Turkey. The black circles around her eyes looked like permanent scarring, and she shook like a leaf all the time. It was an awful thing to see."

"I'm sure. For a week now both my kids have woken up screaming. I think all the TV has been putting bad ideas in their heads."

"I disagree."

"Professor. . . "

"We carefully prodded at her with hypnotherapy. Got her to remember pieces of her dreams."

"And those pieces. . . "

"She dreamed of being in a jungle, running for her life as something relentlessly gave chase. She glanced back, and that glance. . . "

"Yes?"

"Giant, shadowy things. Lots of eyes like clusters of blisters."

"Oh *Christ*!"

"Are you okay?"

"It's been a long week."

"Not sleeping well?"

"Go ahead, tell me it's because I'm secretly remembering the Holocaust."

"I didn't realize you were Jewish. But no, all these ancestral memories we unlocked were truly ancient. You see, every patient we worked with. . . when they had a chance to see their own bodies in the dreams. . . well, it wasn't *their* bodies, understand?"

"No."

"Their dream-bodies were small, furry, and long-armed. It was the bodies of their hominid ancestors, you see? And the environments of those dreams was always the same. Jungles or grasslands. Once in a while, terribly dark caves."

"Professor, against all odds you have intrigued me, but I still don't understand why any of this concerns the President."

"It concerns him—concerns all of us—because all of these people were dreaming from the same period of history, in roughly the same geographic region of Earth. An era when we were australopithecines."

"We. . . what?"

"An apelike ancestor of the human race. A bipedal species living in the Savannah grasslands between two and three million years ago."

"A caveman?"

"A caveman's ancestor. When you think of cavemen, which by the way isn't a very scientific term, you're likely thinking of the popular images of Cro Magnons or Neanderthals. Australopithecines were smaller, furrier, and less organized. That's why they were so easily. . . um. . . hunted."

"You just turned pale."

"This explosion of nightmares—it all originates from the same historical period. When we were australopithecines. When. . ."

"When what?"

180

Project Sargasso Findings

"When there were *other creatures* on this planet. An advanced, unknown species that had evolved to claim the top of the food chain. A hideous life form that built mighty cities while our ancestors picked in the dirt outside their walls."

"You're shaking."

"They used to *feed* on us. They scuttled out of their cities in great bristling hunting parties. They would drive us into the jungles and straight into their webs. You see, the hypnotherapy revealed what our surviving ancestors witnessed first-hand. Being pursued. Being captured in webs, and doing anything—including chewing off limbs—to escape. Watching members of the tribe run straight into glistening, near-invisible webs."

"Oh God."

"We've learned to peel back the memory layers to this grisly dawn, understand? There is an entire chapter of human prehistory lost to us, but it's there inside all of us. We are all descended from the survivors of that age. We all witnessed those *things* coming for our loved ones, their many legs trampling the underbrush, their webs festooning the grasslands and woods. We were no match for them."

"Then why didn't we go extinct?"

"Because one day, our enemies left."

"Left? Where did they go?"

"They ascended into the sky on plumes of fire. I've regressed patients whose ancestors watched their webspun ships climb into the sky. It was only then that the protohuman race could flourish, filling the void left by *their* departure."

"But why leave?"

"We don't know. Maybe the changing climate was troubling to them. Maybe it was political or military reasons. The regressed memories detail butchery witnessed between members of the same hellish species; they were murderers and cannibals, just as likely to put

181

each other on the menu as us. We may never know, but I suspect the chief reason for their flight was to escape a great plague. We detailed memories that described finding them by the thousands as dried husks in abandoned hives."

"A plague? Why do you say that?"

"Last month supplied me the clue."

"You don't think. . . ?"

"I don't think. I know. When the first images of those alien spaceships appeared on TVs everywhere, I had already had those ships described to me! They aren't *alien ships*; they're a homecoming fleet! Remember their greeting to us, broadcast around the world? They promised a relationship between our two species, and as an offering of good will they promised *to cure all harmful diseases* on the planet. They've apparently had time to cure what drove them away. And the instant their ships showed up, something stirred inside our pulvinars. People waking up screaming. They—where are you going?"

"We're going to see the President."

"Finally!"

"You really think they came back to eat us again?"

"I think they want their planet back. Their old food supply is sixty thousand times more numerous than when they departed; we've restocked the old farm, so to speak. And I think they've already won."

"What?! You came here to—"

"—to petition the President to take action, yes. What other choice did I have?"

"The last time they hunted us, we were weak and divided! We've gotten stronger over the years!"

"Sure, but so have they, and they have a two-million-year head start on us, and. . . "

"And what?"

"And they're the ones who are *hungry*. . . "

###

About the Author

Brian Trent's work appears in *ANALOG, Fantasy & Science Fiction, Orson Scott Card's Intergalactic Medicine Show, Daily Science Fiction,* Third Flatiron's *Principia Ponderosa,* and numerous year's-best anthologies.

*****〜〜〜〜*****

Credits and Acknowledgments

Cover image and design – Keely Rew
Podcast production – Andrew Cairns
Readers – Keely Rew, Andrew Cairns, Tom Parker, Leonard Sitongia
Editor and Publisher – Juliana Rew

Thanks to noted horror writer Lizz-Ayn Shaarawi for providing the Foreword to this edition. Her publishing credits include short stories in anthologies such as *Tomorrow's Cthulhu* and *Fairly Wicked Tales*.

*****〜〜〜*****

Discover other titles by Third Flatiron:

(1) Over the Brink: Tales of Environmental Disaster
(2) A High Shrill Thump: War Stories
(3) Origins: Colliding Causalities
(4) Universe Horribilis
(5) Playing with Fire
(6) Lost Worlds, Retraced
(7) Redshifted: Martian Stories
(8) Astronomical Odds
(9) Master Minds
(10) Abbreviated Epics
(11) The Time It Happened
(12) Only Disconnect
(13) Ain't Superstitious
(14) Third Flatiron's Best of 2015
(15) It's Come to Our Attention
(16) Hyperpowers
(17) Keystone Chronicles
(18) Principia Ponderosa
(19) Cat's Breakfast

THIRD FLATIRON
www.thirdflatiron.com